Camo Girl

ALSO BY KEKLA MAGOON

THE ROCK AND THE RIVER

ALA Best Books for Young Adults

ALA Coretta Scott King/John Steptoe Award for New Talent

ALA Notable Children's Book

Bank Street College of Education Best Children's Book of the Year

Capitol Choices List (DC)

CCBC Choices (Cooperative Children's Book Council)

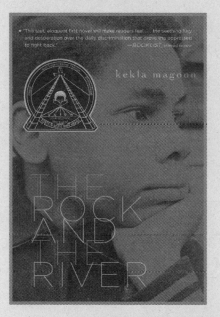

kekla magoon

Camo Girl

ALADDIN

NEW YORK LONDON TORONTO SYDNEY NEW DELHI

FOR ERIC AND SHAWN

ALADDIN

An imprint of Simon & Schuster Children's Publishing Division
1230 Avenue of the Americas, New York, NY 10020
First Aladdin paperback edition June 2012
Copyright © 2011 by Kekla Magoon
All rights reserved, including the right of reproduction in whole or in part in any form.
ALADDIN is a trademark of Simon & Schuster, Inc., and related logo
is a registered trademark of Simon & Schuster, Inc.
For information about special discounts for bulk purchases, please contact
Simon & Schuster Special Sales at 1-866-506-1949 or business@simonandschuster.com.
The Simon & Schuster Speakers Bureau can bring authors to your live event. For more
information or to book an event contact the Simon & Schuster Speakers Bureau at
1-866-248-3049 or visit our website at www.simonspeakers.com.
Designed by Karin Paprocki
The text of this book was set in Cochin.
Manufactured in the United States of America 1012 OFF
4 6 8 10 9 7 5 3
The Library of Congress has cataloged the hardcover edition as follows:
Magoon, Kekla.
Camo girl / Kekla Magoon. — 1st Aladdin hardcover ed.
p. cm.
Summary: Ella, a biracial girl with a patchy and uneven skin tone, and her friend Z, a boy who is very different,
have been on the bottom of the social order at Caldera Junior High School in Las Vegas,
but when the only other African-American student enters their sixth grade class,
Ella longs to be friends with him and join the popular group, but does not want to leave Z all alone.
ISBN 978-1-4169-7804-6 (hc)
[1. Friendship—Fiction. 2. Racially mixed people—Fiction. 3. African Americans—Fiction.
4. Junior high schools—Fiction. 5. School—Fiction. 6. Las Vegas (Nev.)—Fiction.] I. Title.
PZ7.M2739 Cam 2011
[Fic]—dc23
2011003153
ISBN 978-1-4169-7805-3 (pbk)
ISBN 978-1-4424-1722-9 (eBook)

Acknowledgments

I AM GRATEFUL FOR THE DEPTH OF SUPPORT AND encouragement I receive in my life and in my work from a wide range of people and communities:

My parents, who continue to believe in me no matter what, and my brother, who always lets me sit at his table, even though he's so much cooler than me.

My Champagne Sisters, for their advice and for their friendship: Bethany Hegedus, Laurie Calkhoven, Josanne LaValley, and Vivian Fernandez.

The women of my Writers' Group for their constant support and invaluable feedback: Susan Amesse, Diana Childress, Barbara Ensor, Catherine Stine, and Vicki Wittenstein.

The faculty, alumni, and students of the Vermont College of Fine Arts who continue to support me and my work, especially Tami Lewis Brown, Carrie Jones, Leda Schubert, Sarah Sullivan, Cynthia Leitich Smith, and Rita Williams-Garcia.

My agent, Michelle Humphrey, for bringing me to the next level and for introducing me to the greatest cupcakes on earth.

My editor, Kate Angelella, and all the folks at Aladdin/ Simon & Schuster who help transform my manuscripts to hard covers and my ideas to reality.

Thanks to you all!

Chapter 1

CALL HIM ZACHARIAH. HE CALLS ME ELEANOR, BUT the way he says it, it comes out sounding like Ellie-nor.

These are not our real names.

Most people, the sort of people who don't need extra names, can get away with doing simple things like looking in a mirror or taking a bathroom pass out of the cafeteria in the middle of lunch hour. We are not most people.

Z and I have learned how not to see the things we don't want to. It's not that hard, but it makes us seem strange to everybody else. Z, especially, is . . . different . . . from the other kids in our class. Good different, as far as I'm concerned, but the kind of different that makes other people raise their eyebrows and sort of laugh under their breath, as if he's not to be believed.

I've been gone maybe five minutes, but it's too long.

Heading back toward our table, I can almost hear that silly *Sesame Street* song humming in the air, converging on him. *"One of these things is not like the others. One of these things just doesn't belong..."*

Z's in trouble. I'm walking toward him and I see it, know I should never have left him alone, but some things can't be helped. Our eyes lock across the room, and there's nothing in his gaze but stark terror. I should never have left him alone.

Zachariah. Eleanor.

These are not our real names. These are our shadow names, our armor, our cloaks. They are larger than we can ever hope to be; they cause things to bounce off us so we can never be hurt. By anyone. Anything. Ever.

It doesn't always work.

"Zachariah!" I practically scream it, running toward him.

"Ellie-nor," he says, gazing at me with alarm.

These are not our real names, but none of that matters now. For the moment I simply throw my arms up over his head to stop the food from hitting him.

Spaghetti with mystery meat sauce.

Tiny rolling peas.

Vanilla pudding with cookies.

A carton of chocolate milk, unopened, thank goodness.

Z's whole tray overturned by laughing hands. The bulk of it catches me in my shoulders, neck, and back.

Beneath me, Z sits stock still, clean but immobile, gazing innocently at the blank space of the table in front of him. He survived.

This, this is my superpower. My only power, to protect him. He wouldn't understand what had happened. He would pretend not to see. Then he'd make up a story about how he had to crawl through a tunnel lined with bloody, mangled earthworms to get to freedom. He would smile, gooey strings of pasta hanging from his hair, and murmur, "All in a day's work."

Jonathan Hoffman tosses the soiled green tray onto the tabletop. He smiles at me in that *way* that is so infuriating. Is he proud of himself? As if no one else in the history of time ever thought to dump a lunch tray on someone's head.

"Way to take the bullet, C. F.," he says.

My face flushes with rage. I stand with my hands on my hips, ignoring the fact that I'm the one dripping with red sauce and noodles. I am Eleanor, Goddess of Everything, fearless in the face of danger.

"Do you ever get tired of being a gigantic jerk?" I snap.

Jonathan stretches lazily. "My work *is* exhausting," he says, then saunters off to accept the high fives from his table of cronies.

I sink into the seat beside Z and let my head fall onto the table.

"Ellie-nor," he says. "Ellie-nor."

His small hand covers mine. I manage to look up, into his close-to-tearful face.

"Ellie-nor," he says, but I'm not her anymore. Now I'm just Ella. Plain old everyday Ella, the girl with drying pasta goo in her hair, on her skin and clothes. I think some of the peas rolled into my shoe. Little cold mush balls sitting in there.

"You fought the dragon and won," Z says. "You fought the dragon and won."

I smile sadly. "Yeah, I did."

Z taps the table in a drumming rhythm. "Brave, brave, fair lady. You fought the dragon and won."

It'll work for him to pretend. Z's not like other kids. He knows what happened, but he can't admit what it was, what it means about us in the real world. He believes, really believes, that we sit alone at lunch by choice.

I shove my own lunch tray toward him. "Eat this," I say. "I'm really not hungry. Anyway, I have to go change."

Z's hand falls on my sleeve, tugging me to stay with him.

"You would cast aside this badge of honor?" His eyes bug out, incredulous. "You fought the dragon and won!"

Sighing, I unwrap the napkin from his spork and use it to wipe my neck. I left him alone once already today. So, I sit here, watching him eat—he polishes off everything on the tray and some of what fell on the table—until the end-of-lunch bell rings.

People look at me funny as they clear their trays, but it's not only because of the food mess. They'd be looking, anyway. If Z and I were business-minded, we'd build a wall around our table, and a window. We could charge admission for each single peek in. We'd either make a fortune or be left alone. Win-win.

I try to become Eleanor again. Smile as they pass, like I know something they don't. Make them uncomfortable.

"Ellie-nor." Z reaches up under his shirt and pulls out two fluffy rolls. On spaghetti day, you have to pay ten cents extra for rolls. Z does not have ten cents, let alone twenty. He hands me one.

"Thanks," I say, accepting the stolen roll. The lunch ladies don't pay enough attention. Not when we go through the line, and not when we get food dumped on us. I guess it's only fair.

I keep two changes of clothes in my locker. It's important to be prepared for occasions like this. I keep an extra shirt for Z, too, but he'd never actually use it. He meant what he said about the badge of honor. I go along with a lot of his fantasies, but I can't quite get on board with that one.

Z's waiting outside the girls' bathroom for me. He observes my change with large, thoughtful eyes. Then he pushes up his glasses with his pebble of a fist, ready to move on. I tug at the hem of my clean shirt, feeling guilty. Maybe it's a form of surrender, I don't know. I haven't figured it out yet. What the right thing to do is when things fall out of the sky and hit you.

Chapter 2

Z AND I SIT IN THE WINDOW SEAT OF OUR homeroom classroom after school, playing chess. It's our favorite spot. We consider ourselves lucky because ours is the only sixth-grade classroom with a window seat. We consider ourselves even luckier because no one else really cares to sit in it. I wonder sometimes if no one else sits here because they want to avoid seeming in any way like us, but I don't discuss these things with Z. If he knows we're at the bottom of the social order, he doesn't let on.

Fact is, we're the trunk of the popular tree. The very, very bottom of the trunk.

It's okay, though. I don't care about being popular. I'm glad to be friends with Z. He's there for me, every day, and he doesn't ever make fun of my hair or my clothes or the way my skin is dark brown in some places and light brown in others. We exist on a higher plane.

"Knight to Queen four," Z says.

I pull my attention back to Z and his homemade chessboard. I admit that up until this point I may have been looking out the window at the other girls in the playground. After school, the popular girls sit on the merry-go-round without spinning it and listen to each other's iPods, talking about who knows what. Who cares what, really.

"Knight to Queen four," Z repeats.

"I forget what that means," I tell him, but he's already moving the pieces. Z's kind of a genius, is the thing. I can't beat him at chess. I can't beat him at anything, if it involves just cleverness with no element of luck. But I can win at cards and anything involving dice, so the situation's not entirely hopeless.

"Your turn, milady," he murmurs. He's been sitting on his knees, but now he pulls them up to his chest, locking his skinny arms around his shins. He rocks a little, waiting, trying not to smile but failing. He knows he's going to win. It's only a matter of time.

But I'm not the kind of girl who lets a guy win just because it'll make his day. I consider my next move carefully, then reach for one of my castles, sliding it forward two spaces.

Z blows out a long breath. I smile. I may not win, but I'm good enough to make him drum his fingers on his lips between moves, humming to himself—and me—with perfect pitch. His forehead wrinkles like an old man's when he concentrates. The bulbs that are his knees poke toward me, like wishbones covered in butterfly wings.

"Rook to Queen's Rook three," he mutters, narrating my move.

The gibberish of the board space names is lost on me. Z explains it over and over with bug-eyed exasperation, pushing up his glasses. He doesn't really wear glasses, I know. He just likes this pair, likes how they feel on his nose, balanced and important. He found them on the counter at Walmart, where his mother works the night shift.

I pretend not to know the secret. That they live there, too, that he sleeps every night in the corner of the stockroom on a nest of paper-towel rolls. Sometimes I try to imagine the magic of living in the world that way—with all-you-can-drink slushies at midnight and an endless supply of toothpaste. I let it be magic because I can't imagine the other part, what it's like to wake every morning and know that in the course of that day your bed will be sold off for parts.

"Check," he says, and that will be that.

I move my king, because I have no other choice.

camogirl

Z smiles, swooping through his final move. "Check-mate."

"Ella, will you two be walking home today?" Mrs. Smithe stands up from her desk, hands on her hips. She's been grading papers, but I guess she's finished and now it's time to go. There's not a lot I like about Mrs. Smithe, but one thing I do like is how it seems to always take her exactly the length of one chess game to finish grading her papers.

"Yes, Mrs. Smithe."

"Very good. I'd like to close the classroom now, so get along, all right?"

"We're going," I say, nudging Z. He carefully packs up the chess pieces, murmuring words of comfort, like he's tucking them all into bed.

Z lays the chessmen to sleep in one of his four big tin boxes, now empty of their original Altoids. They're bulky to carry around, but while I've known him, there have always been four boxes, always will be four, unless he finds another object to be fascinated by.

He puts the case in his green backpack. Deep inside, his pencils shift. It sounds like a muffled maraca. One box holds his collection of stubby pencils ground all the way down to the metal before he stops using them and puts them in their box. They rattle when he walks, his backpack thumping on the backs of his knees.

The third holds a variety of small, useful gadgets—magnifying glass, magnets, string—I don't know what all. What he keeps in the fourth box is a secret. Even from me. It's sealed with a row of fat rubber bands.

"A prosperous evening to you, milady," Z says to Mrs. Smithe. He pauses by her desk to offer a deep bow. She ought to be used to this by now, but still she frowns, every time.

"Good night, kids."

Mrs. Smithe watches us go, shaking her head with that adult-ish disapproval. Teachers never seem able to accept that Z is reality-challenged. The administration thinks he might be mentally ill, but he's not. And they have no good excuse for putting him in special ed or sending him away, because his behavior in class is perfect, if a bit too formal, and his grades keep him right at the top of the class.

He's a genius, like I said. But most people don't see it because if you don't know him, he just comes across as weird, and most people have a hard time seeing past that.

I brace myself as we enter the schoolyard. Maybe, just maybe, for once, nothing will happen next.

"Hey, C. F. Hey, Freakshow," Jonathan Hoffman calls. He and his friends laugh. They've just come out of JV basketball team practice. They're bouncing the balls, tugging each others' jerseys, and things like that that look all sorts of cool.

Jonathan tucks the ball up under one arm and saunters toward us. We keep walking, but it's a small school, and a small yard. He slings his arm around my shoulders.

"You take care now," he says with deeply faked concern. "Don't wander into the desert, okay, Camo-Face? It's getting dark. We might never find you."

A long time ago I stopped actually hoping that things would ever go my way, but it's still disappointing when they don't.

The chorus of snickers from his teammates is par for the course. I elbow Jonathan hard in the ribs, and he falls away chuckling. I haven't hurt him a bit. I focus all my mental power, willing Z not to do what he's about to. But one thing Z and I don't have is telepathy.

Z waves his hand at Jonathan. "Negatory, old chap," he says. "No expeditions planned for the evening."

The basketball guys howl louder, of course.

I want to fall straight through the earth. At times like this, I wish I could take on a little more Z-ness for myself. I wish I could let the stares and the comments roll off my back like he does. He doesn't hear sarcasm, doesn't accept insults as such.

I glance toward the girls on the merry-go-round. They're laughing, too. I try not to wonder at what. Among them is my ex-best-friend-since-kindergarten, Millie Taylor. She doesn't seem to be laughing. But she's not walking with us either.

The after-school late bus will pull in soon, and I really don't want to end up on it.

"Let's walk," I say to Z. I know my voice is shaking; I just hope he can't hear it.

Z sets off, backpack thumping on his knees. Not quite soon enough, we're out of sight of the school.

"Milady," he says in his serious voice.

"Sir?"

"Life is too short for such a frown."

See, it's not that Z doesn't know what's going on. It's not that he doesn't know what's real and what's not. It's just that he can't stop pretending that the world is a better place than it actually is. If that makes him sick, then I wanna get me some of that flu.

"Yeah, I know." I give him a good grin and try to shake off what the other kids think. None of this is his fault.

Life with Z is not easy, but without him it'd be just me. Alone.

Chapter 3

Z WALKS THE CURB LIKE A BALANCE BEAM. He's found a mangled piece of metal in the gutter, and he brandishes it like a sword. He darts forward, backpack thumping, then stops suddenly, raising his arms in triumph. He looks proudly over his shoulder, and I know enough to clap. He's jousting. And, naturally, he won.

Soon enough, we come to the corner where we part ways. I live to the left. Z heads to the right, into town.

Z lowers his sword and puts out his hand. "Will you be joining me, milady?"

He likes to go to the public library after school to wait for his mom. It's like heaven for him. He dives into a book and won't come up for air for hours. Lately, the best for him are Camelot-type legends of brave knights and fair ladies.

He also likes sci-fi space adventures and anything involving espionage. On any given day, he shows up at school acting like a knight, an astronaut, or a spy. Who knows what he'll fix on next.

Sometimes I go with him, and other times we play at my house. Today I'm too wrung out for any of it.

"It's casino day," I say, which is convenient because it means I need to go and check on Grammie.

Zachariah nods sagely. "I'll leave you to it, then," he says, offering the slightest formal bow. "Milady."

The house is dim, not a lamp lit. I don't like the feel of it. I snap on the kitchen light and look toward the living room. Grammie is sprawled on the couch with her arm covering her eyes. I swallow hard. This can only mean one thing: a bad day downtown.

"Grammie?"

"Ella? Hi, sugar." She lies motionless. A bad, bad day. *Join the club, Grammie.*

I flop onto the couch opposite her. Maybe she's hit on something that makes the icky feelings go away. I sprawl and cover my eyes. It's warm. It's dark. But I can still see everything. Hear everything. Feel everything.

I sit up. "What's for dinner?" One of the things Grammie and I do together that's kind of fun is cook.

She's got loads of recipes stored up in her brain. Doesn't even matter what's there in the kitchen. Grammie can whip up something out of nothing in no time at all. Egg roll spaghetti, taco lasagna, bean dip surprise. We've had a thousand and one whacked-out, spur-of-the-moment meals, never to be heard of again.

"Oh, what does it matter?" she moans.

"Well, I'm hungry, so . . ."

With that, Grammie snaps to. She's off the sofa like a shot. "Well, of course you are, kiddo. Me too, now's you mention it."

We troop into the kitchen. My stomach is clenched, like it's storing up for one big growl. I grab a handful of grapes from the fruit bowl.

Grammie and I consider the options, our stocking feet side by side on the tile. We peer into the pantry, stare into the fridge, survey the countertops for anything inspiring.

"Pizza or Chinese?" Grammie says finally.

"I feel more like pizza."

"Good. Peel me a ten-spot off the wad and make the call."

I order us a large cheese with sausage. We know from experience exactly how much to order so we can thrust a single bill at the delivery guy, tip included, and not have to mess with change. We hate asking for change because we don't like to look chintzy, if we can help it. And let's face it, sometimes we can't. But food delivery shouldn't be one of those times.

The pizza is guaranteed to come in thirty minutes or it's free, so Grammie sets the oven timer. We've never won this game, but it passes the time.

"I think today's the day," I say. Something eventually has to fall in my favor. It's just the odds.

"Nah," Grammie says. "I say he makes it just in time. Winner pays, loser pours."

We shake hands. Then we sit across from each other at the table with plates, napkins, cups, and a bottle of raspberry seltzer all ready and waiting.

"How much?" I ask.

"Seventy-two dollars down." Grammie sighs. "Slots and roulette."

I shake my head. "Gotta learn to lay off the roulette."

"Don't I know it, baby." Grammie smacks the table. "Don't I know it." Then it's like she just snaps out of the funk. "What's up with you?" she says, squinting. "You're looking like a barrel of fantastic yourself."

"I'm fine."

Grammie clucks her tongue the way only old people can. "Fine's no good." She's on her feet now, coming around the table. Zeroing in. She grabs my face.

I try to get away. "Don't look at me."

"Where am I supposed to look?"

I lick her hand. For lack of anything else to do, hoping she'll be grossed out.

Grammie just laughs. "Huh. I wiped your bottom, missy. You think you can scare me off with a little saliva?" But she lets me go.

I hide my face in my arms. "Well, it was worth a try."

Grammie smooths her hand down the part between my braids. She rubs my neck. "Don't let them get to you."

I roll my head to the side. "Who?"

My innocent expression needs some work, apparently. Grammie shoots me a knowing look. "Whoever's getting to you."

"I'm fine, Grammie."

"Oh, you're just asking for the hair, now." Grammie has a fantastic head of bushy white hair, and she will shake it in my face to make a point from time to time.

She grabs my shoulders with both hands and lets it fly. I slam my eyes shut. It's like being whacked with a feather duster, and she smells like Pert Plus. Strands fly up my nose and into my mouth, but by the time she's done, I'm laughing.

Still, I've never been so glad to hear the doorbell ring.

It chimes at the exact same moment the egg timer goes off. Grammie snatches up the money and marches to the door.

I lose my bets.

Chapter 4

DREAD THIS PART OF THE DAY. IT'S EARLY MORNING and I'm still in bed, but I've been awake long enough that I have to pee. It's time to get ready for school. Covers off, feet on the cool ground, scurry to the bathroom. Eyes on the floor all the way.

I can pee with my eyes closed. I'm not super proud of that or anything; I'm just stating a fact. I can do most bathroom things with my eyes closed. Wash my hands, wash my face, brush my teeth, floss. I can comb and braid my hair by feel.

After the fact, I can't be sure. Did I get all the drool stains from the corner of my mouth? Any leftover eye crust? A stowaway piece of spinach in my teeth? A flyaway chunk of hair?

I have to open my eyes. Just for a second, just to check. Just long enough to ruin my day.

Eyes closed, I flush the toilet and glide my way to the sink. The faucet handle is where it always is. So is the soap. I wash my hands and face, then grab for my toothbrush.

Eyes closed, I fumble for the toothpaste. It's not there. I pat around the counter. My chest seems to fill with steam as I come up empty, again and again.

Grammie's onto me now. She keeps moving things. Not just a little, but someplace ridiculous, so I'll be forced to look before I find it.

I lean against the counter, hating her.

Twice now I've covered the bathroom mirror with brown paper, but Grammie won't let me keep it up. She spreads her tiny toes on the tile and stretches up to tear it down, piece by piece. I don't like the way she looks at me after the fact. Like I'm not good enough, or brave enough, to see the truth when it's in front of my face.

She doesn't understand.

I open my eyes, glancing everywhere but straight in front of me. The toothpaste is planted nose down in the Kleenex box. Gee, why didn't I think of that?

When I'm done brushing, there's nothing left to do but check my work. *Eyes, teeth, hair. Fine? Good.*

I close my eyes again, but not for long. The damage is done. The girl in the mirror looks back at me. Curious. Sad. Ugly.

I get why people stare. It's like the train wreck: You don't really want to look, and you know you shouldn't, but you just can't help it.

I take a deep breath as I step into the hallway.

There are these moments, see, when I'm far away from anything reflective, when I'm caught up in whatever I'm caught up in, and I feel myself smile, and I imagine someone seeing me and liking what they see.

Chapter 5

WHEN IT'S JUST THE TWO OF US, Grammie listens to NPR morning talk radio. I try to tune out the yammering as I drag my backpack into the kitchen and slump at the table. Grammie's sitting with a short stack of cash, a tall pile of coupons, and the shopping list, muttering, "Another day, another dollar."

I try to look on the bright side: Mom comes home tonight.

A bowl of shredded wheat and half a grapefruit are waiting for me. When Grammie's not looking, I sprinkle extra sugar on both. Mom prefers the fake stuff, but she hides it when she's away so that Grammie doesn't ditch it. Grammie tried to ban it from the house at first, insisting that it's going to cause me to grow a second head one day, but Mom says Grammie really hates it because her first name is Splenda and she's radically pissed that they stole it.

"Five minutes, kiddo," she says. "Get a move on."

But I don't. Clearing my plate takes all of ten seconds. There's no big rush. Anyway, I don't care about getting to the bus stop early anymore.

My ex-BFF Millie and I now have a fifteen-minute friendship. It starts at about 7:40 when we wait at the bus stop together. We share a seat on the bus and look over our homework together. It ends at about 7:55, when we get off the bus and Z is there waiting for me.

That's when Millie runs off to be with her new friends, and we all pretend like it's no big deal. We used to hang out after school, the three of us. Now, well, I don't really know what Millie does with her time.

She's waiting already at the corner between our houses. Her golden hair is tied in a ponytail at the base of her neck. I stuff back my disappointment. Today is not the day.

"Hi, Ella."

"Hi, Millie."

She's still a nice girl, but we used to braid our hair the same way every day. We would decide the night before what color ribbons we were going to wear so that we could match.

"What did you get for number sixteen?" she says, holding her math homework out to me.

"That's what I got," I say, glancing at the page.

The other sixth-grade girls wear their hair down, or in a ponytail. I can't do that. My hair swells into a big puffball if it's not braided, and it's not like I don't have enough problems as it is. Anyway, I like braids. I liked Millie's especially, because her hair goes halfway down her back, and they were like gold silken ropes that would glide through my fingers. Amazing and smooth.

"Did you know," she says, "Rick Small and I are going together."

"Where?"

She blushes. "You know. Just *going*."

"Oh. That's great."

Millie likes braids, too. She always thought it was impressive that mine could stay in place even without a ribbon. One time she even said she wished her hair could do that, though I can't imagine why.

"Cass passed a note in third period yesterday, and he checked yes."

"Well, then, he's not as dumb as he looks."

"He is cute, isn't he?"

I hold back an eye roll. The bus rumbles up the street. Millie slides her fingers through her ponytail, staring at the curb and maybe thinking about Rick Small, he of the big chin and tiny brain. I would have passed the note if she had asked me.

Do you like Millie Taylor? __ *Yes* __ *No* __ *Maybe*

Right now I'm leaning toward a big fat NO.

Still, every morning I pack an extra pair of ribbons in my bag that match mine. We don't make the plan anymore, so when she changes her hair back, how else will she know what color to use? I come ready, but I'll never tell her this until the day she shows up with braids.

Chapter 6

I N THE LONG RUN, IT'S HARD TO PICK OUT ONE day from the next. When it's happening, it seems like each day is worse than the last and will never, ever end.

I climb off the bus behind Millie, who jets off before I can even say bye, and Z's always waiting for me. He comes to school early because he gets to eat the free breakfast they provide for poor kids. Afterward he usually hovers by the corner of the building, trying not to get noticed by anyone very big. Usually this works out, because Jonathan Hoffman's mother drives Jonathan to school, and he tends to arrive at the very last minute.

Today Z's sitting at the corner there, hunched under his backpack, looking small and reading a book while nibbling on a biscuit the size of his fist.

"I had two," he says, giving me a guilty glance over his glasses.

"It's okay." I sit down beside him, not caring that he didn't save me a biscuit. He's really very sweet about things like this. Maybe that's how I justify not telling anyone about the things he takes.

I would be allowed to eat the free breakfast too, but Mom says we don't need handouts. At least, not anymore. One year, the year Daddy got sick, which was most of second grade and part of third, I had to take the school breakfast. Every morning that year Mom shook her finger in my face and said, "Tell them thank you, and don't get used to it."

Now we have Daddy's life insurance, plus Mom got her job with the train company, and Grammie moved in, so we're okay.

Z licks crumbs from the creases of his hand, not okay.

The days do blur together, but every once in a while something happens that stands out. We're in math class, the period right before lunch. My desk is at the edge of the classroom, unfortunately close to Jonathan Hoffman, who likes to lodge small objects in my hair when no one but his friends are looking. He's gotten very good, and I don't always notice, until I see Brandon or Martin or Will across the way, turning purple from trying not to laugh out loud. Then I have to decide—leave it there, not knowing what or where it is, or run my hand over the back of my head to remove the paper clip/penny/gum/gum wrapper/spitwad/you-name-it, and let them know they've got to me. Or, worse, reach for it and not be able to find it because it slipped in between the seam of my braids, or is something piecewise and subversive like eraser dust that I'll need a mirror and tweezers to remove, which is their favorite victory of all.

I grip the edges of my desk. Today we're so far, so good. Brandon and Martin are only folding notebook paper into tiny triangles and flicking them across my desk at each other. I can deal with this, no problem. Though I will never understand how they actually get away with it. Can't Miss Miller hear the tiny, repetitive *whoosh*es and *thunk*s? Why doesn't she ever turn around at the moment when they're making their victorious gorilla faces at each other, with two fists in the air?

Any field-goal attempts that don't make it across my desk, I confiscate. Occasionally a bad punt skitters to a stop on my algebra notes, and I grab it. They hate this, but so far they're not clever enough to try to use it against me. They interpret it as acceptable losses, not an escalation of tension. They will not negotiate for the safe return of their prisoners of war.

I've caught five already. *Flick. Skid. Grab.* Make that six. Brandon curses and tears out a new sheet. I smile to myself. Mom says not to worry. Smart people always win in the end. I bend closer over my notes.

That's when I feel the first tug. Jonathan's fingers on the bottom of my braid. My stomach clenches. What will it be today?

As it turns out, today it will be nothing. As it turns out, today is a day of small miracles.

A noise behind all of us causes Miss Miller to turn away from the chalkboard midsentence. Jonathan releases my hair at once. Brandon sits up straight, fumbling for his neglected pencil.

"Ah, hello, there," Miss Miller says brightly, raising her attention to the doorway at the back of the classroom. She extends her hand, motioning someone forward. "Class, meet our newest addition. He's just moved here. Bailey James."

The next five minutes pass in an absurd slow motion. For real. I mean, Zachariah tends to be the dramatic one, embellishing our daily life with Shakespearean enthusiasm. I just let things happen as they will. Not today. Today the world tilts, and when it rights itself—if it rights itself at all—I am left standing askew.

Chapter 7

TURN MY HEAD ALONG WITH EVERYONE ELSE TO get an eyeful of the new kid. Bailey James. At first glance, I blink hard in his direction.

I'm floored.

He's tall, wearing a Utah Jazz jersey over a T-shirt and jeans. And he's black! Deep copper-skinned, big-lipped, flat-nosed black! And gorgeous.

I quickly look away. But I can't help it. My gaze is drawn back as he waves at the room.

"Hi, everyone."

"Hi," they chorus. Me, I'm speechless. Bailey James. I say his name in my mind a few times. First to myself, then as if to others: *Yeah, Bailey James. You know, the other black kid.*

The other black kid.

Bailey James is looking around the room. I haven't had

time to worry what he'll think. I'm too shocked, too busy looking, to try to hide my face. His glance lands on me, moves on. Returns. Moves on. Returns. My heart is all but leaping.

Then his face breaks. Bailey James smiles at me. Actually smiles. Then he gives this little nod as if to say, *Yeah, I'm here. You're not alone.*

I lay my head on the desk, in case I start to cry.

Chapter 8

I TRY NOT TO THINK ABOUT CERTAIN THINGS VERY often. Some are real things, like how very skinny Daddy got right before the end, or how much money Grammie has lost in the casino over the years, or how much I miss Mom when she's away. Some are made-up things, like what it would be like to have a big brother who could beat up Jonathan Hoffman and five of his friends all at once, or what if Grammie really hit the jackpot and we got rich overnight.

Or what it would be like if there was another black kid in school.

For the rest of the period I avoid looking toward Bailey James, who Miss Miller assigns to the empty seat way across the room from me. When the bell rings, I grab up my books to make a break for the cafeteria. I make it all of two steps before I find myself staring at the words "Utah Jazz."

Swallowing hard, I look up. Bailey James has come all the way across the room and is standing in front of me.

"Hi," he says.

I stare up into his face. "Hi."

It cannot be me speaking. My voice is locked, behind the huge knot in my throat.

And that's the end of it. Jonathan Hoffman swoops in, slinging his arm around Bailey's shoulder. "Hey, man. Welcome to Caldera. You going to go out for basketball? I'm on JV."

Jonathan steers Bailey away from me, into the center of his group. Jonathan, staking his claim.

"Yeah, yeah," Bailey says. "I play."

He does not look back. Jonathan's friends crowd around him, and their conversation quickly morphs into gibberish talk about balls and stats until they fade into the hallway.

I am shattered, speechless. Whatever was about to happen, however small, is finished. My eyes burn. Hatred for Jonathan Hoffman threatens to drown me. These boys have everything, take everything. I don't know how they do it. I don't know what more they want. But I'm sure they'll get it.

"Ella," Miss Miller says. "Are you going to lunch?"

Garnering a smile for her, I put one foot in front of the other.

Chapter 9

Z GOES STRAIGHT TO THE LIBRARY AFTER school. I don't let him entertain other options; I just want to go home. I run most of the way there.

Bursting in the door, I shout, "Mommy?"

She's sitting on the couch in Daddy's big red tube socks, flannel pants, and a tank top, sealing envelopes of our bills and watching *General Hospital*.

"Hey, baby." She reaches out her arms to me and I fly into her lap. She hugs me so tight and I try not to take any deep breaths so she won't let up. If I never move, it'll be okay.

"You're getting too big, missy." She groans, patting my side to end the hug. I move but curl up on the couch with my head against her. She rubs my back and my shoulder and kisses my cheek.

"I saved you the stamps," she says, stroking the edge of my hair. I like to peel the stamps and stick them. Return address labels, too.

"I'll do them," I say, but for now my eyes are closed.

"Tell me what's new, Ella," she says, muting the television. "I don't like missing half of your week."

Mom works for the train company as a steward on the long-distance passenger trains. She wears a blue uniform with red pinstripes. Las Vegas to Chicago takes two days each way, with three days off in between. That means she's gone four days a week, and home for only three. But that's how we pay all the bills. It's also why Grammie has to live here, to help take care of me.

"Where's Grammie?"

"I sent her shopping," Mom says. "She was only too happy to go."

I smile to myself. I'll bet she wanted to go, just to get away. Sometimes Mom and Grammie don't get along very well. I'm not supposed to know it when they fight, but I don't know who they think they're fooling. Grammie said once that they're both trying to love me enough to make up for Daddy being gone, and all that love can make a house get hot. I'm not sure that's what she meant to say, because she tried to take it back after she said it, but maybe it's a little bit true.

"She had the coupons out this morning," I say.

Mom squeezes my shoulder. "Lasagna bake for dinner, okay?"

I burrow against her stomach. The good me would protest. Lasagna bake is a lot of work—it takes a whole hour and a half. I know she's tired since it's the first day home, but I do love lasagna bake.

"Okay."

"You didn't tell me what's new," Mom reminds me.

My happy place is suddenly not so happy. I sit up. "Nothing's new. School. Homework. Same old, same old."

Mom studies my face. She knows what I look like, and she loves me anyway. Then again, she kind of has to. She's stuck with me.

"Same old, same old, huh?"

"Yeah." I don't think this constitutes lying, even though I could say other things. *There's a new boy in school, and he's black. His name is Bailey James, and he looked at me. He came over to me and said hi, and we almost talked.*

She would smile. She would ask me if he's good-looking. Maybe she would worry a little less. *I almost made a new friend, Mom.*

Almost doesn't count.

Chapter 10

STRANGE THINGS HAPPEN IN A HOUSE OF women. Last week, for instance, Grammie climbed up onto the roof to put new tiles on a patchy spot, and there is nothing funnier than a ninety-five pound, sixty-four-year-old woman flapping around up on the eaves like a bird. The whole time, loudly declaring there's no good reason to pay a man to come and do something just because he's a man when she could do it herself perfectly well. I was like, "Go, Grammie!" on the inside, but mostly I was just lying in the grass, laughing at the sight of her.

Another time Mom burned our dinner on the stove because she was in a mood and not really paying attention to what she was doing. Grammie and I sat at the dining room table, smelling it, and playing rock/paper/scissors over who had to go in and help her. In the end neither of us went in; we just kept increasing the number of matches. Best of three, five, seven, nine. We made it to best of thirteen before Mom came to the table carrying a five-pound bar of chocolate and a half-gallon tub of honey vanilla-crunch ice cream. Grammie and I looked at each other and shrugged. Mom sat down, and we proceeded to eat it all.

There are some times when Mom gets cranky like that, and I think we're coming up on one now, because she's rubbing her belly and watching afternoon soaps, plus she's wearing Daddy's old socks, which is what she always does when she's sad or out of sorts.

"I'm back!" Grammie's voice echoes in the hallway. "Hop to, kiddos!"

Mom and I do not move. We will, of course, but we have to work up to it.

Grammie sweeps in, hands on her hips. "I did the buying, you do the lugging." She drops into her recliner, shoes off and stocking toes to the ceiling before Mom and I even get all four feet on the ground.

"We're going," I say. Mom heads for the kitchen, which means I get the lovely task of bringing in all the groceries. But if these are the dues that earn me lasagna bake, I'm in.

"How attached are we to this soapy business?" Grammie mutters, fingering her remote control as I pass.

I pat my stomach and shrug. Grammie rolls her eyes and puffs out her cheeks. I know this look. When I got my first monthly a few months ago, Grammie rolled her eyes to the sky just that way. "Lordy Lou. Here we go." Then she took me out for ice cream. "Eat up, it's the end of the world as you know it. And the beginning."

I run to the car. Three trips out and back and all the bags are in. Mom's slicing veggies in the kitchen, and Grammie's pretending to doze in her chair. I crawl under the dining room table with my school books and get started on my homework. When the days are rough at the edges, it's best to stay quiet and out of everybody's way.

After a while Grammie's snores echo through the house. So much for pretending. I wonder what Grammie'd be doing right now if she wasn't here with us. She used to have her own house, a few miles away where we would go to visit on Sundays. She sold it to help pay Daddy's hospital bills. I heard her say on the phone once that when I'm old enough to mind myself, she's going to move to her own apartment. Something closer to the Las Vegas Strip, so she doesn't have to take the bus all the way in to the casino every week.

I keep that a secret from Mom, though. I'm not sure if it'd make her happy, or make her worry.

The smell of lasagna bake soon gets my mouth watering.

Mom calls me to set the table, then yells, "Splenda, dinner's ready."

Grammie pads into the kitchen. "No need to break my eardrums over it, Keisha. I'm here."

They exchange a Look.

I think, deep down, they like each other. It's just that when we're all together, they remind each other of Daddy. At times like this, his not being here gets really big in the air.

Mom's Look wins. Grammie waves a hand to be done with it and peels off toward the table.

Mom says Grammie's a hard nut to crack. I guess it's true because I once saw a soup can fall out of the cupboard onto her head, and she didn't even say "ow." She just grumbled about having to bend down and pick it up off the floor where it landed.

Sighing, Mom reaches over and strokes my hair. She frowns, sliding her fingers deeper. She extracts something from my curls, a long silver sliver that looks like a dull needle.

"Ella, why is there a piece of lead in your hair?"

It's a refill stick for a mechanical pencil. I snatch it out of her hand. "I was looking for that." I swallow it in my hand, squeezing so hard it snaps in two, pricking me. In my darkest dreams, I'll use it to poke tiny holes in Jonathan Hoffman's jugular.

Chapter 11

Z AND I ESCAPE THE NEXT DAY WITHOUT much torment. It's not just me—everyone is distracted by Bailey James's presence among us. He's brought a whole heap of cool to Caldera Junior High. His smile is a light show you can't look away from.

Twice I catch him looking my way. Our eyes meet, which should be nothing, but it's something.

It's something.

At lunch Bailey sits at the table with Jonathan Hoffman. He doesn't try again to talk to me. I'm ready in my mind, though, just in case. He'll come over and say hi. I'll say hi back. Then I'll brush the end of one braid over my shoulder, all casual. *What's going on?*

What happens after that depends on what he says in

response. But no matter what, I'll have a great comeback, something witty, so he'll laugh and I'll get to see his smile up close. Or maybe I'll be super cool and glamorous, a movie heroine. I'll be like, *Is that so?* or *That's to be expected*, while shooting him a sultry gaze.

On second thought, I don't know what sultry really looks like.

"Ellie-nor."

"Hmmm?"

"Ellie-nor."

"What?" I draw my attention back to Z. He's sitting right next to me, looking at me, rubbing his hands in smooth circles over the tabletop.

"Will milady offer the knight her leftover fare?" He speaks quietly, unevenly.

Lunch is almost over, and my tray is half full. I push it toward him, wondering why he didn't just go ahead and pick some food off my plate. I obviously wouldn't have noticed.

The end-of-lunch bell rings. Z stacks my picked-at tray on top of his empty one, because chivalry is the code of knighthood. Usually, both trays are empty. Always. We don't throw away food.

I'm about to ask Z why he didn't finish, when Jonathan, Brandon, and Bailey go by with their trays. Bailey looks at me and smiles. That makes three.

Then they're past us, thumping their trays on the side of the trash cans and tossing them in the service window.

Z stands expectantly, holding our trays.

"I could look sultry," I inform him.

He stares at me for a moment but says nothing, then walks to the window and deposits our trays. Thrusts them down a little too hard, if you ask me.

Z sticks close to my hip as we step out into the hallway, dodging the crowd flow as the seventh-graders thunder into the cafeteria for their lunch period. He holds the hem of my T-shirt as we make our way back to class.

Chapter 12

I PRESS UP AGAINST THE LOCKERS AFTER FINAL BELL, waiting for Z to situate things in his backpack and get his lock secured just so. He tucks away his boxes, one by one. We'll go play chess now. These last moments in the crowd are all that stand between it being just the two of us for a while.

Millie and her friends glide by without a glance in my direction. I try to act like I didn't even see them, though, in case they're actually looking at me.

It's not always so easy to go unnoticed. Jonathan Hoffman fires finger machine guns at me. He blows the "smoke" off his fingertips, then puts one hand to his brow, squinting as if he can't tell for sure whether he hit me—I'm so hard to see with my camo face. The depths of his cleverness continue to astound me. Not. I shoot him my most withering look.

Behind him, Bailey James walks alongside Jonathan's buddies. I wonder if he saw and if he thought it was funny. So much for us ever talking.

The hallway flood slowly eases, and we are among the last few kids at the lockers. Z fumbles with his backpack zipper, then finally looks up, ready.

"Milady," he says, with a nod.

"Sir," I respond automatically, but my mind is pretty much following Bailey down the hallway.

I don't want to always be the freak. I didn't used to be. It happens in tiny stages. One day things are normal. The next, they're on their way to not. Someone shows up in a desert camouflage T-shirt, and Jonathan Hoffman realizes it looks a lot like my face. Millie stops coming over every day. Then she stops coming over at all. Last year we would have been walking out the door together, the three of us. I don't know exactly what happened. I don't know exactly what changed.

I don't like what we've become, these fake friends who don't always notice each other.

"Milady," Z repeats.

"Yeah."

We walk toward Mrs. Smithe's classroom together. I don't look back. I'm done with the rest of them. Z is my friend. We are apart. No one else knows what it's like to lose something like what we have lost. And he's always been there for me, even on my very worst day. . . .

I slipped outside to wait. People had been coming by the house day and night to hug us and bring casseroles. Our family was all up in the house, which isn't very big for so many people.

My shoes dangled from my fingertips because, all things considered, barefoot is better. I put my toes in the grass, because I knew better than to lie down in my new black funeral dress. It had a row of pretty red roses across the middle. The shoes, black patent leather with a red bow and a two-inch heel. I'd never been allowed to wear high heels, but the day before, Mom just nodded when I picked them out. They weren't very comfortable.

The screen door screeched open. "It's time to go," Grammie said. "Get those fancy new shoes on, and let's hit the road."

Instead, I let the shoes drop onto the porch, and ran.

I knew the path well, which was good because I couldn't see real well right then. The tears that stung my eyes blocked out everything. I climbed the rope ladder to the tree house. Piles of cushions and picnic blankets caught me as I flung myself inside.

It didn't matter how many times they told you it was going to happen. It's still the worst thing ever.

I didn't know how long I'd been there when he came. I heard his little footsteps *shush*ing through the grass. The rope ladder swung and the wood creaked, just so. I closed my eyes.

He crawled up next to me. The fabric of his suit brushed against my bare feet.

When I finally looked, he lay there with his face next to mine, brow wrinkled, unsmiling. "Hey."

"Hey."

"I guess you know they're looking for you," he said quietly.

I pinched my eyes shut again. "I'm not going."

"Okay," he said, very serious. "Want me to send in the stunt Ella?"

I didn't know where it came from. The smile. "Yes, please."

Mom called out my name. Right from the backyard, but she sounded so far away.

"I can't go," I told him. "I really can't."

He studied our fingertips, lying side by side, then pressed them together. "So, what if we stay here, and we send someone else in our places."

"What are you talking about?" I knew I had to go. There was no way out; I was just trying to act like there might be.

"Yeah." He sat up, getting excited. "You can be a super-hero or a princess or . . ."

"Superhero princess?" I said, liking the sound of that.

He clapped his hands. "Yeah, yeah. You be . . . Princess Eleanor. I'll be a knight. Sir—"

"Zachariah," I filled in, out of nowhere.

He smiled, halfway bowing toward me. "At your service, milady."

I sat up, smoothing my braids with my fingers.

"Now, let me rescue you from this terrible tower."

With stealth and speed, we scaled the rope ladder, jumped the "moat," and galloped through the yard, as if on horseback. Mom was so relieved to see me that she didn't notice our whispered messages back and forth.

Our alter-identities lasted all day. Our little secret. Whenever anyone spoke to us, we would say something cryptic but in character, like "Indeed, good sir," or we'd invite them to the "banquet." Z was all into reading the King Arthur legends, and he knew so much about knights and ladies and how they talked and acted.

And when it was hard to pretend, we sat quietly and tried anyway. Z made up funny medieval stories about the old people at the service and did a hilarious bit of miming where he pretended to be stalking Mr. Pattison's really bad wig like it was a wild animal. It did rather seem to have a life of its own.

Part of the time I was too sad to laugh out loud, but I

laughed in my head. Z held my hand while Millie's father and then my uncle stood up and talked about Dad.

I will never forget that.

Z took my sad day, the saddest day ever, and turned it a little bit magic. He knows how to do that. Sometimes, every once in a while, I get to see the world through his eyes. It's a much better place. That's why he tries to live there.

After chess, we walk home. At the corner where we split, I say, "Headed to the library?"

"No," Z says, then stands, waiting.

"Oh. Do you want to come over and play?"

Usually, these are complicated decisions for him. Escape vs. companionship, duking it out in his mind. He tilts his head. Maybe there's an actual boxing ring, and he watches, waits, to see who'll come out on top on any given day. Today we need each other too much.

Today, without so much as a wistful glance toward the library, he smiles. "Lead the way, milady."

Chapter 13

WHEN MOM'S ACTING CRANKY, JUST about anything goes. Grammie stays in her room a lot to avoid crossing Mom's temper, thus keeping her usual busybody self out of my hair, and Mom sits on the couch in the afternoons watching the sort of cheesy television that causes her to reach for tissues from time to time.

It's because of this and only this that Z and I get away with building the catapult.

We clatter around the pantry and come up with a plan. Using miles of masking tape, we lash the mop handle to the broom to the Swiffer sweeper, and by then it's decently long enough that we think we have a shot of getting Millie's cat to fly all the way over the woodpile.

It's not as mean as it sounds. We've secured him in

a padded basket, all cushy with a blanket and copious amounts of bubble wrap. To be totally honest, I'm not sure this is the best plan, but Z's taking the name "catapult" really literally at the moment.

"Cat-a-pult," he murmurs as we experiment with using a beach ball, a lawn chair, the barbecue grill, or my lower back as a fulcrum. I'm on my knees with the pole leaning over my back when Grammie sticks her head out the window.

"What in the name of creation!" she shrieks.

I scramble to my feet. "We're fine, Grammie!" I wave up at her.

Five seconds later she's standing over us, huffing and puffing from the little sprint she just did.

Grammie takes Z by the sides of the face. "You're going to hurt the cat," she says softly, studying him. "Do you want to hurt the cat?"

"Fair maiden," Z says, laying his small hands over hers. "This fierce, brave jungle cat that we have captured cannot be harmed. Have you seen him in his wild form? He leaps from tree to tree with ease, this magnificent hunter."

"Cats always land on their feet," I translate.

"Not when they're trussed up in bubble wrap," Grammie says. She kisses Z's forehead, and shoots me a sharp *you-know-better-missy* glare. "New game."

o o o

Pretty quick after Grammie gives us the talking-to, Z gets tired of playing. It's a lot of work, coming up with an idea like the catapult. And very disheartening not to get to see it reach its full potential.

We lay in the grass beside our failed experiment. We position ourselves the usual way: head to head, with our feet sticking out in opposite directions. So we're ear to ear, really.

I know what's coming next. Z blows out a quick, short breath. Then he sucks in a chestful of air and starts blowing loudly.

I wait until I think he's going to have to breathe or die before I suck in a breath of my own. Blow it out in a long, slow *whoosh*. We go back and forth as long as we can until we are both gasping for breath and not laughing becomes too hard.

"Wind tunnel!" Z shrieks, rolling until his cheek touches the grass. A few blades poke into his nose and he sneezes, which just makes us both laugh louder. When we're all laughed out, we look up at the clouds. Today they're few and far between. The sky is blue-white and almost spotless.

Z murmurs something to himself. I glance at him out of the corner of my eye, not sure if I was supposed to hear, and answer. He stares up at the sky, and I wonder, not for the first time, how it is in his mind.

Millie's cat, now free, skulks in the grass around our bodies. Why he's not running for the hills, I don't understand. Glutton for punishment, I guess. Or maybe it really wasn't so bad, what we almost did.

I look at Z, lying there, all innocent and thoughtful. All wrapped up in his imagination, wherever it's taking him. The cat steps on his belly, and he gently strokes its ears.

There's a fine line between things you can get away with and things that are actually wrong. The catapult episode is a small case. There are bigger cases.

I'm talking about times when the real world and Z's world don't line up and he doesn't seem to see it.

"We shouldn't have tried that," I tell him. "Putting Gorbachev in a bubble. Cats can't fly."

Z laughs. "Cats can't fly, milady. Cats can't fly," he repeats.

I get that feeling all of a sudden, that desperate tugging feeling that I want the game to be over, just for a minute. I roll toward him. "Come on, you know it wasn't very nice."

Z rubs Gorbachev's head. "To tame the wild beast is no simple feat."

I grind my heels into the grass. "It's Millie's cat," I say. "'Wild' to him is Mrs. Taylor's garden."

Z glances toward Millie's backyard. Maybe he's looking for the garden. Maybe he's looking at the tree house—

the one we both sometimes forget isn't ours anymore.

I try again. "Are you sad?"

Z jerks his chin back, pointing his face to the sky. He gazes at the fluffy, floating clouds.

"It's just us," I whisper. "You can talk to me, when it's just us."

I know he's listening, but I guess he doesn't want to come back to Earth. I try to content myself with seeing things his way. Grammie says sadness doesn't last forever, but with Z and me it's sometimes hard to see that.

It's quiet out here, until suddenly it's not. A strange sound from inside the house, or on the other side of the house. Sort of a pinging, kind of echoey. I sit up, listening. Z sits up too, gathers his backpack, and slides it onto his shoulder.

"Do you want me to have Grammie drive you to the library?" I say. Sometimes we do that. Usually when it's raining or cold, which isn't all that often, but we've been known to do it just for the heck of it too.

Z shakes his head. "No, I will ride." By which he means horseback, by which he means walking. He climbs to his feet. "Good day, milady Ellie-nor."

"Good day, Zachariah."

He takes a shortcut across my backyard and into Millie's. The cat wanders vaguely after him, but I don't worry, because it won't leave our yards. It doesn't like the feel of cement compared to grass.

I'm quite ready to go inside, but there's something going on, something nagging at me. It's the sound. The echoey, pinging sound that is both strange and somehow familiar. Then it stops and there's another sound, a sort of metallic *thunk*, but dull. Then it's back. *Ping*. Echo. *Ping*.

What is Grammie up to now? I skip around the house to the front yard.

"Grammie—" The word is out of my mouth as I'm coming around the corner and, oh, how I wish I could take it back. I'd just melt right into the side of the house and pretend I was never there.

It's not Grammie.

Really, really not.

It's a boy. I stand, exposed, as he catches the basketball he's been bouncing in my driveway and turns.

Not just any boy. Bailey James.

Chapter 14

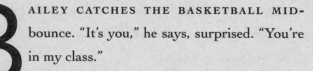AILEY CATCHES THE BASKETBALL MID-
bounce. "It's you," he says, surprised. "You're
in my class."

I put my hands on my hips, feeling reckless.
"You're in my driveway." Those words were never part of
the plan.

Bailey cringes, looking, I don't know . . . guilty? "You
have the only basketball hoop in the neighborhood," he
says. "Do you mind?"

I contemplate. If it were Jonathan asking, I would say
no, just because I can. Instead, I shrug. "It was here when
we moved in."

Bailey frowns. "You don't play?" He dribbles hard in a
fancy pattern, spinning with his feet. So cool.

"I don't even own a ball," I say.

Bailey grunts like this is a deep sacrilege. "Want me to show you?"

I don't do sports. Really don't do them. But I find myself saying, "Yeah, okay."

Bailey grins, and I feel myself blushing. This is so not going to go well. Why did I say yes? He takes two steps closer, still smiling, and I remember why.

"So, tell me, Ella," he says. "How much do you know about the sport of the gods?"

He knows my name. I didn't tell him. Did I? *Hi. Hi.* That was it. Until just now. I never told him. But he knows. Which means he must have asked someone. Which means he was thinking about me. Somewhere, somehow, for just a second.

I turn my hands up. "I know it's called basketball," I say. "And it tends to be orange."

Bailey flips the ball up onto one finger, spinning it artfully. "Well, then we have our work cut out for us."

"I'm at least twenty minutes away from being able to do that," I say, pointing.

Bailey laughs, actually laughs, at what I just said. His smile gets better the longer he wears it. I don't get tired of looking.

Bailey teaches me to dribble, guard, pass, check, and shoot. I throw the ball up over and over, but it just refuses to go into the basket. Bailey never laughs when I miss, he just goes, "Good try," or if it wasn't, he gives me pointers. He laughs a lot of the rest of the time, though, sometimes close to my ear. I like the sound of his voice.

He explains the rules, and we try to play one-on-one, but obviously I'm no match for his actual skills. He must be bored with me. He's really patient, though. I wonder why he's not still at the school, playing ball with Jonathan Hoffman and his cronies. That would be more his speed.

Instead, he's here. I try to guard him, but he's really fast and gets by me every time. We don't keep score, because what's the point, but he gives me plenty of turns. There's a part where his hand is on my back, guarding me. I duck, spin, stop, aim, aim a little longer, shoot.

The ball swishes through the net, making my first basket ever! I jump and clap my hands, screeching, "Yes!"

Bailey pumps his fist in the air. He hugs me with a hard fist-thump on my back. I'm suddenly very aware of my training bra. We pause in the hug, then spring apart. The basketball rolls to a stop against the pole.

"Um," Bailey says.

"Um," I say.

"Um, that was really good," he says.

"I never made a basket before."

"Yeah? Cool."

Bailey fetches the ball and holds it in front of him. I'm not sure if he's about to check it to me or if he's using it as a shield. Knowing me, I'm going to go with shield. I take a step back.

The sky's grown dusky, almost dinnertime light. It's a little funny that Mom and Grammie haven't come to call me in yet.

"Can I ask you a question?" Bailey says.

Anything. "Um, yeah, okay."

"How come you hang with that little white boy?"

So this is how it ends. Still, I was lucky. I had one whole afternoon with Bailey, all to myself. A whole afternoon living some other girl's fabulous life.

I tilt my head, innocent. "Everyone here's white."

Bailey shrugs. "Yeah, I get that, but why *him*?"

I search for something to say besides the real reason. "Someone has to look out for him." We don't know each other well, so I figure half truths are okay. Saying it also makes me seem . . . whatever the girl version of chivalrous is.

"Yeah, I get that," Bailey says.

No one gets that. Maybe he's just being nice.

"I gotta go," he says a second later. Confirmed: He's just being nice.

"Bye."

"Bye."

I call after him, a shade less than desperate. "You can use the hoop anytime."

Bailey looks back over his shoulder, gives me a full-arm finger point. "Count on it."

Chapter 15

SLIP INSIDE AND LOCK THE FRONT DOOR. MOM and Grammie are tripping all over each other in the kitchen, working on dinner. It seems like they just got started.

My stomach rumbles.

"No dinner?" I say. "What have you been doing?"

Grammie waggles her eyebrows at me. "Oh, honey. What have *you* been doing?"

Mom chokes back a laugh and smacks Grammie with a spatula. "Hush. Leave the child alone."

My heart thumps, eyes narrow. "Why?"

Grammie turns all matter-of-fact on Mom. "Keisha, they were right there in the driveway, for all the world to see. She has no choice but to tell us all about him." Grammie winks. "That's what we women do."

"There's nothing to tell," I mumble. "He's just a boy from school. He won't be coming back." It hurts a little to say it out loud.

Mom and Grammie Look at each other. Mom smiles at me.

"I know a thing or two about men," Grammie says.

"Splenda, please," Mom groans.

Grammie waves her fork, undeterred. "I know men, when they're coming and when they're going," she says. "That one'll be back."

I make a silly face at her, because, well, that's just what I do. I make the silly face, but underneath, I'm really, really hoping she's right.

Chapter 16

A S IT TURNS OUT, THE FOURTEEN HOURS between when Bailey leaves and when I get on the bus to go to school in the morning are plenty of time for me to work up a story in my mind. Here's how it goes: I jump off the bus, smiling. Bailey's there, waiting for me. He grabs my hand, tells me how much fun yesterday was. He thinks I can be great at basketball. He's been thinking about it, and I'm really quite a natural. I just need a little polish, and who better to teach me than him? He will be over every day from now on, to show me things. Not only that, but he'll walk the halls with me, holding my hand, not allowing me to exert myself, so my strength will be saved for the game.

A lot can happen in fourteen hours. Even more can not happen.

I jump off the bus, smiling. And who is waiting for me but Z. His hands are sticky with icing as he holds out a cinnamon roll to me.

I take it, but all the while I'm looking around. Bailey is nowhere to be seen. I keep looking, though. Z and I sit at the corner of the building until the bell rings. Nothing.

We stand up, bracing ourselves for the day ahead. Closing my eyes, I try to swallow the knowing for sure. It's just another day. Nothing special.

I open my eyes and suddenly, there he is. Strolling up the sidewalk with his backpack slung over one shoulder, like all the cool kids do. We don't do that. We carry our bags on both shoulders because one of Z's books informed us that anything less is bad for your posture and spine alignment.

But it's the kind of day where things might be different. Of its own accord, my left shoulder eases out from under its strap. I catch the full weight of my bag on the right side. My whole body adjusts, falling automatically into a very cool swagger. Huh. Is that all it takes?

"Ellie-nor," Z says, patting my loaded pack with his hands.

"Stop it. It's fine," I snap, and he lets go. Draws back his arms like a startled turtle. I didn't mean to be rough with him. I really didn't.

Z shadows me as I take two small steps forward. I smile at Bailey.

Seconds pass. He waves. Five fingers in the air. Finding me. I give five fingers back. Then he's swallowed. Basketball players Kurt, Rick, Max, Brandon, Miles. Jonathan Hoffman hops of out his mom's car, right on cue, and jogs to join them.

Their chatter is loud; so is their laughter. Bailey's right in the thick of it.

Bailey and his effortless cool.

Bailey, surrounded by new friends.

Bailey, who hugged me just last night, now untouchable.

The warning bell rings. "Not to be late. Not to be late," Z mutters. He takes off toward the doors, and I have no choice but to follow. It is just an ordinary day.

Z holds the door open for me. It's heavy, and he struggles under its weight. The chivalrous thing, always.

I glare at him, unnecessarily. I let myself get carried away. It's always been fun, his games. His imagination. Now I see the other side. I see why he dives into his head and never comes up for air. I see how bad it hurts when even the smallest bubble of a dream is punctured.

We hurry to class, making it well before the final bell. I hang my bookbag on a free peg. Another pair of hands hangs a bag beside mine. Dark brown hands. I can't help it.

I look up. Bailey gazes back at me. It feels like forever, but I barely have time to take in a breath.

Maybe I'm going to speak. I don't know. Or maybe I'm going to wait for him to speak. He gives me a small smile, no teeth, then moves away, slides into his seat. Without a word.

I blink back my sadness. I don't have to wonder any longer. Yesterday was just an accident, a fluke. A one-time-only. Today is just an ordinary day. I try not to look across the room, but a couple of times I slip. I never catch him looking.

Bailey's status as new kid puts him high in the leaves of the popularity tree. Thing is, leaves can fall and still be leaves, but the trunk is the trunk and it stays where it stays.

Chapter 17

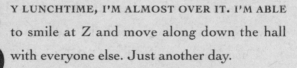

BY LUNCHTIME, I'M ALMOST OVER IT. I'M ABLE to smile at Z and move along down the hall with everyone else. Just another day.

When we get to the cafeteria, something in me gets a little reckless. I hang back while Z heads for our table. I'm planning a different route. I'm going to be Eleanor, just for a moment, just long enough to do something brave.

I walk past the table I usually avoid like the plague. Bailey's just settling in, alongside Brandon, Miles, and Ken.

My plan, so well thought out, is this: I'm going to look Bailey James in the eye, say hi, and keep on walking. The part that's not so well thought out is: Why?

I squeeze between two chairs, coming out right beside him. The simple greeting balances on the tip of my tongue.

I stall.

They all look at me. Bailey, eyes warm and curious. Jonathan, sneering and cold.

"Bug off, Camo-Face."

"Whoa," Bailey says. "What did you just call her?"

My face flushes hot. I spin away, but Bailey's hand falls on my wrist. My tray rattles.

Jonathan glances around, puzzled. "What, her? That's Camo-Face."

It's one of those moments when the sky is falling. I try to push it back up in my mind, but it's already crashed over me, and I can't breathe or think or speak. I tug free of Bailey's grip and wade through the atmosphere, away.

"Uncool, my man. So uncool." Bailey's voice follows me.

And Jonathan's. "Hey, where you going, dude?"

I can't help but look back. Bailey's standing up. He starts to lift up his tray. Jonathan glances at his buddies around the table. He grins nervously. "It's just a joke, man. An old joke."

I stare at him, appalled. I can't think of anything worthy to say in response, so I just start walking away. The names I call myself in my head are so much worse than Camo-Face.

Out of nowhere, there's Bailey. Walking beside me with his tray.

"Sorry," he says. "I had no idea he was that big a jerk."

Bailey took my side! My heart leaps, with nowhere to go. I don't want to be needy girl, sad girl, loser girl. I am Eleanor. Strong girl. It-all-rolls-off-me girl.

"Whatever," I say with a sniff.

"Really." He's dogging me around the room. "Guess I picked a bad crowd to start off with."

I brush one braid over my shoulder, elegantly. "It's no big deal. Forget about it."

Bailey shrugs. "I've been looking for a reason to move tables, anyway. You can come sit with me," he offers. "Over there." With his head, he points toward the long table where more of the popular kids sit. The boys: Kurt, Rick, Max. And the girls: Cass, Megan, Kelly, Liza. Millie's there too. A table I've always wanted to sit at. A table of no one who will talk to me.

Max motions to Bailey, who tips his tray like, *Yeah, I'm coming*. He glances at me, expectantly.

"I have a table," I say. "Where I sit."

Z's there already. Alone. Eyes wide behind his glasses. Fork in hand, unmoving.

Bailey and I look into each other's eyes. My heart throbs. My skin flushes warm. He looks all over my face, and I resist the urge to run, to hide. He doesn't look away. This is going to be it. The moment when everything changes. He'll come sit at our table, and we'll no longer be just two, but three. He doesn't look away. And then he does.

"Okay," he says. "Well, I guess I'll catch you later."

I haven't even blinked before he's weaving away through the tables.

I slam my tray down next to Z's. He begins eating silently, leaving me to wallow in my own shattered mess.

It's not clear to me what's happening. What's clear is, I should have left well enough alone.

Chapter 18

FTER THE LAST BELL, Z'S WAITING, AS
usual. His chess box is in his hands, and he's
practically twitching with excitement.

I hate to do what I'm about to. "Do you
mind if we skip the chess for today?"

He takes the news well, but I can see it knocks him
down. "Milady?" he whispers.

"I just want to go home, okay?" I push past him, ready
to leave. By myself.

Z walks with me out the door. I'm moving faster than
he likes to, but he keeps pace. He says nothing more to me,
but after a few blocks he begins muttering to himself.

"I'm sorry," I say. "I'm just tired." Z's baleful gaze
washes over me. I think maybe he can read my lies, but he's
just not equipped to hear the truth. This day is breaking

me. I want to lie alone, in my own dark and quiet room, and forget any of it ever happened.

Z says nothing aloud. In his muttering I make out, "Covert mission. Full stealth. Enemy territory."

We get to the corner, where we part, and he takes his turn without so much as a "milady." He skulks along the bushes as though trying not to be seen.

I didn't think this day could hurt any worse. I was wrong. Even Z's closing the door on me. His knight fantasy is about us together. His spy fantasy is about him alone.

Chapter 19

THE DAYS WHEN THINGS CHANGE ARE THE hardest. I want to disappear through the scrub brush and melt into the desert. My skin *is* like camouflage, swirls the color of sand and the color of bark, and I know how to crawl on my belly like a marine and how to make myself blur like a shadow. Z taught me that. Once upon a time, before everything got messed up.

I get home, and Bailey's sitting on my front porch. I blink to be sure. Scrub my hands over my cheeks. I can rub away the tears, and I'll have to settle for that because what I'm really hoping for is so out of the question.

"Hey, girl."

"What are you doing here?"

"Wow. Don't sound so happy to see me." His smile is a million degrees hot.

"I—You surprised me, is all. Where's the basketball?"

"Left it at home. Want to hang out?" he says. I stand in the driveway staring at him. I don't know what to do with a boy who isn't Z.

"You and me?"

He grins. "Turns out we live near each other."

This day has been so much heaven and hell colliding. I cross my arms, desperate to hold it all in. "Yeah, I guess we do."

Bailey studies my face. Can he tell that I've been upset, confused, crying? I hope not. We don't really know each other well enough to notice things like that. At this rate we never will. He can't keep showing up after school like this. He must have better things to do.

"I hope you're not letting those jerks get to you," he says, leaning against my top step.

"Who *are* you?" I blurt. Because he's not like any boy I've ever known or heard of.

"Bailey James," he says with a matter-of-fact smile. He is very boy and very cute. My heart actually starts going a little faster. Weird.

"Bailey James," I repeat. I don't want to have to survive

another day like today. The uncertainty. I don't want to have to wonder. But he came here, after all, knowing this time that he'd find me here. And there's something about his smile. "Okay, Bailey James. Let's hang out."

Chapter 20

'VE NEVER RIDDEN ANYONE'S HANDLEBARS BEFORE. I have a bike of my own, right there in the garage, but when Bailey says, "Let's go for a ride. Hop on," how am I supposed to counter that?

It's not so easy to balance, but Bailey says we don't have far to go. My toes are planted on the little nuts that hold the front wheel spokes in place. I grip the bars hard beneath my behind. The bike wobbles every so often, and I have to stifle my every yelp and scream.

When Bailey says, "You okay?" I chirp, "I'm great!" After all, I'm the bold lady Eleanor. If only Z could see me now.

"We're here," Bailey says. His knuckles graze my hips as he lifts his hands away. I jump off, flexing my fingers.

Bailey chains up his bike beside the local park. Some

other kids from school are hanging out on the swings. They wave when they see Bailey. The boys don't seem to notice me, but the girls whisper furiously.

There's this awkward moment when we get to where they are and no one says anything. Bailey turns like he's going to introduce me, which if he does, I'll just die because I've known everyone here since before kindergarten.

"Hi," I say, before he can say anything.

"Hi, Ella." Cass is the first girl to speak. "How are you?"

The ice, the thin, thin ice I'm standing on, has broken and, surprise, surprise, I'm not even wet.

"I'm fine," I say. "Hi, Kelly. Hi, Liza." The two other girls smile at me. We're all uncertain, we are all on tiptoes, or maybe it's just me. Gearing up, I turn to the last girl. "Hi, Millie."

"Hi, Ella."

"Um," Max says. "We were about to go get some shakes at Willy's. You want to come?"

We parade down the street to the local diner. Willy is about a hundred years old, but he can make anything you can imagine you might want to eat, and make it good.

The others start crowding into a booth. It's one of those half-moon benches that's designed for five or six people, but there are nine of us. I hesitate, thinking I will have to be part of the small group that's sent away. Cass nudges me, and I flop forward, thumping into the booth. She sits down right next to me, prodding me to slide along. She flicks her fingers at me, and I scoot, scoot, scoot, until I've come around the U and find myself shoulder to shoulder and thigh to thigh with Bailey.

Too Close. Bailey and I are sitting too close. His shoulder leans against mine on one side, but I can't move away because Cass is right there on the other. Not that I want to move away. But I do, because when he turns his head, his face will be right next to mine. He'll see me up close, and that can't be good.

A waitress brings a tray of water glasses and slides them around in front of us. There isn't one for everyone, so I don't reach. Not until I know what's going on. The waitress whips out her notepad and stands expectantly by the side of the table.

One by one, the guys order chocolate milk shakes. The girls order diet root beer floats. I've always been a fan of milk shakes. Strawberry-banana.

The waitress stares at me, snapping her gum.

"Diet root beer float," I say.

The waitress nods and spins off. Her sensible shoes make a little squeak on the tile floor. I wait for some reaction from the others. I'm pretty sure I ordered right, but still.

No one is looking at me. Cass and Liza are comparing lip gloss flavors from their purses. Bailey and Max are getting riled up talking over the fourth quarter of last week's Knicks–Lakers game.

No one is looking at me. Kurt methodically folds his place mat into a paper football. Millie pretends to read her place mat, but I can tell she's hiding a smile, possibly because she's sitting right next to Rick. Rick and Kelly fight over the sixth and final glass of water, sending most of it splashing across the table. Cass rolls her eyes and throws both of our napkins into the fray. Bailey turns his head toward me and grins. It feels right, so I smile. But I still feel like I'm waiting, like there will be some great moment of realization when they all see me as one of them or else point me out as the poser I am.

I've infiltrated. The thought goes through my head quickly, and it makes me giggle a little. Cass glances at me and shrugs her shoulders like, *What?*

I shrug too, searching for a plausible excuse. Finally I lean over and whisper, "Bailey's . . . cute."

Cass giggles. She whispers back, "Yeah."

I giggle again, 'cause it's allowed, and Cass can't read my mind. I've infiltrated the popular people. In a weird way, Z would be proud.

o o o

We step outside the soda shop, and the most amazing thing happens. Bailey slings his arm around my shoulders, all casual. "Give you a ride home?" he says.

A thousand yeses bubble up in my throat, get caught.

Out of nowhere, Z is there. Watching us. Tears rolling down his fragile cheeks.

Chapter 21

I'VE MADE A MISTAKE, A TERRIBLE MISTAKE.

The soda shop is right across the street from the library. Z stands on the library side of things, down at the curb, glaring at us. From this distance, he looks so small. No jacket, no backpack. Just his ratty T-shirt and jeans.

How long he's been watching us, there's no way to know. Or what he's thinking.

Our eyes meet. He takes fleeting steps backward until his back is pressed against the outside wall. He sidles around the corner, almost out of sight.

I shrug out from under Bailey's arm. "I can't," I say. "There's something I've gotta do."

"Oh." He digs his hands deep into his pockets, stares at

me. I don't think he noticed Z, so he'll think I'm ditching him, but what else can I do?

"I want to," I whisper. "I just can't."

"Okay," he says. "Hey, let's go somewhere else after school tomorrow. Just you and me."

My heart flutters. "Okay."

Bailey turns to catch up with the others, who've moved on down the street. All except for Millie, who lingers, looking after Z. And Rick, who lingers, looking after Millie.

I meet her eyes, but I don't know what I'm telling her, or what she's asking. It's been a long time since we could read each other's thoughts. I don't know what it means, her hesitation. It can't have very much to do with loyalty.

"See you tomorrow," I say, because maybe she just wants to be let off the hook, and anyway, I'm not about to ask her for anything. Not anymore.

Chapter 22

As soon as Millie and Rick turn their backs, I go after Z. I tail him all the way around the building and back into the library. He stalks through the children's section and into the boys' bathroom before I can catch up.

I see what's happening. He's trying to be artful. I go someplace that he can't; he goes someplace that I can't.

So I wait.

I sink onto the hall carpet, rest my head on my knees. He has to come out eventually. I don't know what I'll say to him; I really don't. I hope he saw that I was with Millie, at least. I'm the one in the middle, the one who's supposed to hold us together, like I promised him I would. Maybe he'll believe that I'm trying to put us back the way we were.

We used to be neighbors, the three of us. Millie on the

corner, me next door, and Z the house after that. One big backyard, no fences. It feels like such a long time ago, but I remember. There were nights when Mom and Daddy would put out the grill, and they'd have Z's parents and Millie's parents over while we played. We'd camp out in Millie's tree house, run through my sprinkler, or ride Z's tire swing until we fell over, dizzy. A few summers ago, before everything changed, we all three spit in a bowl, then we pricked our fingers and dripped blood in it and wrote out the words *Best Friends Forever* and signed our names with a paintbrush.

Now, it's like we draw a line around ourselves: No trespassing. Millie put up glass and Z put up bricks and I put up brown paper, which seems like it'd be easy to tear, but it isn't.

"What are you dooooing?"

I lift my head. A four- or five-year-old kid stands in front of me, with Kool-Aid lips and touseled hair.

"Whatever I want."

He reaches out his grubby hands, as if to touch my face. I flinch away.

"You're weird."

Now, there's a revelation. "Will you tell the other boy in there that I said to come out please?"

He stares at me.

"You have to pee, right?" I snap.

Nodding, he uses his whole body weight to lever open the door. A few minutes later he comes back, skipping by me without so much as a glance.

"Hey, did you tell him?"

He gazes at me, indignant. "No one's in there. I went all by myself."

Chapter 23

"WELL, AREN'T WE MOODY TONIGHT," Grammie says.

I pick at my mashed potatoes, glaring at her. "Leave me alone." This day has been a total mess. I'm so ready to call it a wrap.

"Okay, so . . . I guess dinner's over." Mom says. "Clear your plate."

"Whatever." I start to get up.

Grammie waves a fork at me. "You'd better get out of that funk, little missy. This here's a happy homestead."

"Yeah, well, the freak is feeling funky tonight."

Mom silences Grammie with a Look. "Honey, you know how I feel about you saying things like that."

I grab my plate and glass and make a break for it.

In the kitchen, Mom takes me by the shoulders. "Hey,

where's my girl?" She wraps the end of my braid around her fingers. "It's my last night home this week. I'd like to spend it with you."

I let her hug me without saying anything. Everything that comes to mind is mean. I don't want her to go, and that's the least of my problems.

Slinking back toward the living room, I meet Grammie on the warpath.

"Ella Baker," she says, raising her eyebrows at me.

"Grammie—" I'm not in the mood for this game.

"Ella Baker!" she insists.

"Namesake number one," I mumble. "Civil rights activist. Registered black voters in the Jim Crow South at great personal risk."

"Thank you. Ella Fitzgerald."

"Namesake number two. Jazz singer of the Harlem Renaissance. Beautiful voice, beautiful person."

"Ella Cartwright."

I stand quiet. Grammie gazes at me pointedly.

"That one's me."

"And what do we learn from this?"

I all but choke on the words. "I'm named for great and beautiful women; I am a great and beautiful woman."

Grammie nods triumphantly. "You are indeed. Now, was that so hard?"

Yes. "I'm going to bed."

"Brush your teeth," Grammie calls after me.

The lights are on in the bathroom. It's no more horrible than ever, but no less.

Mom's face appears in the mirror, over my own. She's so pretty. Her dark, smooth skin is flawless. I see her, but I don't see where I came from.

We look at each other. Then we look just at me.

"Would you believe I forget sometimes?" I whisper.

Mom strokes my hair. "Honey."

It's true. Like today. I was sitting by the bathroom, waiting for Z, and my mind was on everything but how I look. The little boy staring at me brought it all back. The forgetting makes me free, for a moment, but it isn't worth it in the end. If I could just know it all the time, it wouldn't come back like that, and surprise me.

"I'm a freak."

Mom hugs me from behind. "Anyone who can see will see you beautiful."

I close my eyes and try to make it true, just for a second.

Chapter 24

Z DOESN'T SHOW UP FOR SCHOOL THE NEXT day. I get off the bus in the morning, and no one is waiting. All day, I'm sick with worry. Worse, I'm all alone.

Z doesn't skip school. He just doesn't. When he's sick, he comes anyway, and they let him lie in the nurse's office all day.

After school I leave the building at a dead run.

I race in through the library doors. Mrs. Baskin, the afternoon librarian, is sitting at the checkout desk reading a thick paperback.

I slap my hands on the desk and lean in. "Please tell me he's here."

"Yes."

"Where is he?"

Mrs. Baskin gives me a pointed look. "Where do you think?"

"It's not my fault," I blurt.

Mrs. Baskin slides a bookmark into her book. "What happened, Ella?"

There's no time to explain.

I find Z lying on the floor beneath shelf 327.12 (spy books), balancing a thick tome over his face. He's cleared the shelf and scattered all the books around him. *Burn Before Reading. A Century of Spies. The Know How Book of Codes, Secret Agents & Spies. The Art of War.*

One look and I know. It's bad, really bad. Worse than I thought.

"Go away. I'm undercover," he says.

"As what? A bookend?" I wave my hand at the large pile of books beside him.

He lowers *The Encyclopedia of Espionage* long enough to glare at me.

"Z, come on. What's wrong?"

"Sometimes you just need a day off," he says in a dull voice. He's repeating something I told him once. Grammie lets me take the occasional mental health day, but Z has always found this objectionable.

"I was worried about you."

"I can take care of myself," he says, rolling away from me. "Solo mission."

Sighing, I plop down beside his head. He fingers the spines of the books, pretending not to see me.

"I looked for you yesterday. To say I was sorry." Part of me isn't really sorry, though. I had a fun time with Bailey, and it wasn't planned. It wasn't how it must have looked to Z. Who still refuses to look at me.

"I said I'm sorry, okay?" I snap at him. It's not fair to be mad, but I am. I was really worried, and now it turns out he's fine—just staging a protest. But Z's always been there for me, in his way, and there's a lot to be said for that kind of loyalty.

I try to be there for him, too. On his sad days. Like he was for me.

The saddest day for Z was about a year ago, when his dad left. Right after that, they lost their house. I went over that day to help him pack his room. I came in and found him sitting on the bare mattress, clutching the Altoids box, the fourth and most secret box with all its rubber bands in place. He was crying.

I took one look at the room and knew this was a desperate situation. His things were scattered around in disarray, open boxes everywhere waiting to be filled. I wanted to cry too, because everything looked hopeless and torn. But I knew what I had to do.

camogirl

93

"Sir Zachariah," I said. He raised his chin to look at me. The tears dripped off it like drops from a leaky faucet.

"Milady Ellie-nor," he murmured. I wasn't sure, but his eyes seemed to brighten. He dried his cheeks on his T-shirt sleeves.

So I garnered my best Lady Eleanor face. I brandished my imaginary sword and leaped around the room, vanquishing all kinds of foes into cardboard boxes. For a while Z just sat there watching my antics.

There wasn't much left, truth be told. Some toys and clothes and small random objects, things that he wouldn't be able to keep in his new life anyway, as it turned out. Apparently his dad had taken away some of his furniture and things and already sold them. I found out he even took away their real chess set, with the tall ceramic pieces and carved wooden board, which is why Z later made his own.

Later, I heard Mom and Grammie talking about it. Mom said when Z's dad lost his job, he went into Las Vegas to try to win some money. He never came back.

Neither did Z. His sad day became a sad week, sad month, sad year. At the rate he's going, maybe a sad forever. Or maybe he's simply got everything figured out. The hard things just keep adding up, and it's easier to try to be someone else.

I lie on my back beside him, filling up the aisle. He

turns the pages silently for a long time. When he scrunches toward me so that his back is up against my side, I know we're going to be okay.

I know him so well. I know what a good heart he has. He's always there for me and we'll always have each other, and I know, I know, all of those things are more important than anything else.

Chapter 25

TRUDGE HOME WELL BEFORE SUNSET. ONCE, Z AND I lost track of time reading the encyclopedias and I forgot to go home in time for dinner. Grammie showed up at the library at six thirty, stamping her feet and swinging her elbows, basically hopping mad and worried. I wouldn't have thought her hair could get any bigger, but that day it was like a mushroom cloud. I'd rather not go through that again.

I round onto my block, and there's Bailey. Spinning and jumping around in my driveway with the basketball.

Oh, no.

Oh, god.

I race toward him.

"What gives?" Bailey bounces the ball at me and I catch it. "I've been here like an hour."

"I'm sorry," I say. "It was kind of an emergency." I've really done it now. I shove the ball back to him. Hard. But who I'm mad at is me.

Bounce. "You totally disappeared after school."

Shove. "I'm sorry. Really."

We send the ball back and forth, a nonsensical little battle. Then it stops. The moment of silence opens wide.

"No big deal, I guess." Bailey rolls the ball between his hands. "Is he okay?"

I drop my book bag in the grass. "Do you want to play ball, or what?"

I can't talk to Bailey about Z. I wouldn't know where to begin. And even if I could, would he really care, in the end?

Bailey spins the ball up on his fingers. "Yeah, that's why I came."

"So let's do it."

He checks to me. Dribble, dribble, block, shoot. We don't have to say anything much beyond "Your ball," "I'll get it," and "Nice shot." I like these moments, being together, all close, without having to work on what to say or not to.

We try keeping score, which is kind of a train wreck because in only ten minutes it's already like 30 to 3. Between plays, he looks at me out of the corner of his eye, like he's trying to figure me out. I figure he can see me looking back.

We take a water break at 80 to 11. I think he's actually going easy on me.

"If I get to a hundred before you get to fifteen, I win," he says.

I laugh. A little too hard. "I'm really giving you a run for your money."

It all seems worth it when he smiles. "For sure."

At 99 to 14, I can no longer tell if he's rigging it, though he's suspect. I have control of the ball. He steps back, allowing me my final shot.

"I'm glad you did come," he says suddenly.

"I was always going to come," I lie. "I just didn't expect it to take me so long." Maybe it's not even a lie. After all, I live here.

"So, he's okay, your friend?"

I take a moment to aim, shoot. "Everything's relative," I say. The ball wobbles against the rim for a while before falling out.

"I hear that." Bailey retrieves the ball, smiles at me. He barely glances at the basket as he makes his shot.

I applaud. "Surprise! You win."

He grins. "Close game, though." In a manner of speaking.

I hold out a pretend microphone, "We're live with Bailey James, after his stunning upset victory over Ella Cartwright. How do you feel?"

"Hungry," he says, not really playing along. "It's gotta be dinnertime."

My microphone hand falls to my side, all awkward. "Oh, right." Things had been looking up, but now we're back. Leave it to me to mistake a dorky impulse for something cool and funny.

"I'm sorry I was late," I say.

"It's cool. We can try again tomorrow."

He doesn't say it like a question but it is. One big question mark hanging over us, over me.

"Why don't I leave this here," he adds, extending the basketball to me. We're arms-plus-arms' length apart. I'd have to reach out and take it. But I can't.

I see it really clearly now. The line. What happened just now, and yesterday, and the day before with Bailey, that's not me. This is me. The line makes me tell small lies, like saying I'm sorry when what I really am is embarrassed, confused. If I had it to do over, I'd still run after Z.

Z's my first priority. He has to be. He needs me. And I need him.

There's a circle drawn around me, and only Z knows the way in.

Chapter 26

I DIDN'T TAKE THE BASKETBALL. BAILEY GAVE IT to me.

I just stood there, and he kind of stared at me, then said, "Okay?" as he bounced it to me. I caught it, but that's all.

Now it's Saturday. I wake up and run downstairs. The basketball is still there, where I left it, rolled into the corner of the front porch. I don't know what happens next.

It wobbles a little when the wind blows. Just a little. But I step outside to get it, bring it inside where it's safe. There's bound to be a good spot for it in the garage somewhere.

I don't know what it means to have a basketball that belongs to Bailey but lives here. Is he trying to make an every-day plan?

I have every-day plans already, and they're with Z. I don't see how I can do both.

There's an empty spot on the tool shelf, between the box of nails and the pile of sandpaper. I slide the basketball into place, study it. It sits there, listing forward a bit, like it's not sure it wants to stay.

I pat its rough burnt-orange skin. At least we agree on something.

I didn't take the basketball. Bailey gave it to me, and when he figures that out, he might just come back long enough to take it away.

Chapter 27

BAILEY RIDES HIS DIRT BIKE OVER THE lawn, instead of coming down the street and up the driveway. This is called a hypotenuse, which we learned yesterday in math.

"It's a good thing you don't have a driver's license," I say. "Lawns everywhere, beware."

He grins, hopping off the seat and leaning the handlebars down onto the grass. "Efficiency."

It's Saturday afternoon. He's wearing a New York Knicks jersey.

I come off the porch and head for the side of the garage, carrying my small bag of trash. He can't know I was waiting. Hoping.

He pokes around a bit, looking, then fetches the basketball from my garage. "You got a bike?" he asks. "There's someplace I want to show you."

"What?"

"Oh, no. I'm not telling."

He sticks the ball under his arm, hopping back on his bike. I yell to Grammie that I'm going for a ride, and we take off down the street. Bailey rides hard, glancing back at me occasionally, but every time I'm right there, keeping up. This, I know how to do.

We make a wide left turn beyond the edge of our subdivision. The desert stretches out all around us, and Bailey leads me down a well-trampled path of scrub dirt, every rut of which is all too familiar. I know where we're going. I slow my riding.

I brake, nearly toppling over. "Wait," I say. "I don't want to."

Bailey circles around me. "What? Don't want to what?"

"Can we go back? Please?"

"Naw, man. This is so cool."

He's excited, thinks he's discovered something. My old worn-out world is brand-new to him. He grins, and I do what I can to smile back. He's excited, and maybe it's just for today. Someday, this place we're going will be old to him, and me along with it. Maybe this is all I get.

"Okay," I say.

"Yes." He rides on eagerly. I follow. I only have him for a little while longer. He's the kind of boy for whom there's always something new. I don't know how I know this about him, but I feel how true it is.

The sky stretches out, and the world drops away in front of us. The mesa in the late afternoon light takes my breath away. It always has.

I've only ever been here with my dad.

I let my bike fall over and I step to the edge, where a thick ridge of rocks rises up, just before the cliff that falls into the desert below. I turn my face to the billowing clouds. *Hi, Daddy.*

When I come around again, Bailey's taking in the sights, and I'm one of them. "You've been here before." He doesn't seem disappointed.

"Yeah."

"I don't know much about you," he says thoughtfully.

My pulse speeds up. Why? "I don't know much about you either."

Bailey shrugs. "You know I can handle a ball. That's pretty much all there is."

I sit on the rocks with my legs dangling toward him. It is a beautiful spot. I don't want to be sad here, now, but I am.

"I thought you were a Utah Jazz fan," I say.

"No, sorry." He lies flat on the ground, nearby. "Are you? I didn't think you had a team."

"I don't. You wore it to school a few times, so I thought . . . you know."

"Utah's the closest team to here," he explains. "I figured most kids would be for Utah. Or Phoenix. I have a Suns jersey, too."

"So, you're really a Knicks fan?"

"No." Bailey grins. "Don't try to guess my team. I have all the shirts."

Bailey James, man of mystery.

"Where did you live before?"

"Delaware. Before that, Pensacola. Before that, um, Seattle?"

"Wow."

"I'm used to being the new kid," he says, tossing the ball up and catching it. "We move around a lot."

I can't imagine it. I never remember living anywhere but in this house in this town. Every inch of this place is part of my story.

"How come?"

"Military brat." He shrugs. "You get used to it."

"So, you might be leaving?" I felt it. I did.

His expression goes funny. "Naw. Probably not for a while this time."

"Your dad or your mom?" I say.

"It's just my mom."

"Oh. She's in the military?"

"No." Bailey catches the ball, holds it. "I don't like to talk about my dad," he says.

"Me either," I whisper.

For a long moment we rest there, locked in something silent but strong, held fast by whatever sadness is hanging over us. I don't know about his dad, and he doesn't know about mine, but there's a second where it's like we do know. The line we draw around ourselves sort of breaks open. For a moment, we're a figure eight. Everything else is outside, and it's just us. In.

Chapter 28

SUNDAY MORNING I FIX MY OWN BOWL OF cereal for breakfast. The house is quiet, which is odd because Grammie's not the type to sleep in. I knock on her bedroom door, but she's not there. I find her in the garage, tinkering under the hood of the car.

"What are you doing?"

"Well, we need an oil change," she says, showing me the fresh line on the wiped-clean dipstick. "You wanna ride into town with me? Need to stop at the Walmart, too."

"Yeah?" I say, hesitant. That's where Z's mom works.

Grammie fixes on me with hawk eyes. "Your new friend coming to play today?"

"No." Bailey says he has something to do on Sundays. A family thing.

"Well, then, let's go, kiddo." Grammie swats at my behind with the grease rag until I hop into the backseat.

Fine.

There's one of three places where I can always find Z. The games and puzzles section, the snack bar, or automotive.

Today he's in automotive. I almost don't notice him. He's sitting on the floor, staring at the tall piles of tires, holding one of his boxes in his hand. Box 4. The special box. The secret box.

He has a small satchel beside him, smaller than his school bag, no doubt for the rest of his boxes.

"Hi," I say.

Z flinches, startled. He clutches the box to his chest, like armor.

"Milady," he murmurs.

I fold my legs beneath me, across from him. "Zachariah."

He slides the loose box back in the bag with the others. "Ellie-nor."

We look at each other. It's one of those moments where we're both trying to make sense of things. And probably coming up with different answers, which isn't how it used to be. One plus one doesn't always equal two, for whatever reason.

"We missed some games this week. Do you want to make them up?" I say.

Z fingers the edges of his bag. He says nothing but reaches in and extracts the box of chessmen. He knows which box it is by feel, even though they're basically identical.

He lays it between us.

"Okay," I say. This is good. I draw a makeshift chessboard on some computer paper out of Z's bag.

If we don't talk, things seem to be how they always were. We move the chessmen up and over. Z wriggles his fingers with dramatic flair.

I play along, try not to think about what's wrong with this picture. How I have to remind myself not to say anything, because anything I say will make Z upset. I try not to think that it's wrong, all wrong. I should be able to talk to my best friend, real words, not part of the game.

"Your move, milady."

"Sorry, sir." I hop a knight.

He grins, pushing up his glasses. I'm about to lose gloriously, and Z is approaching glee. I realize I've missed seeing his face light up over the small things that make him happy.

"Checkmate!" he cries.

"You got me good," I say, groaning dramatically. He laughs.

I start resetting the board. Z joins me in lining the little men up again, but when everything's set, he pauses.

"Milady, shall we consider a feast before battle?"

"Okay," I say. "What do you want?"

He considers. "Pop-Tarts."

"You wanna get them, or should I?"

"Milady must away to our rationed stores. I shall guard the soldiers," he says, stroking his king's shoulder lovingly.

I roll my eyes. "Well-laid, sir."

The grocery section is about as far on the other side of the store as you can get from automotive. I leave Z, walking the big center aisle that runs the width of the store. My sneakers glide over a slick spot on the floor, giving me a little dance-shimmer effect. Which I decide to try again. And again, as I make my way toward the snack aisle.

I snag a box of Strawberry Pop-Tarts off the shelf. It's not stealing as long as you save the box so you can scan the bar code and pay for it afterward. Z's mom works here, so she can do that, no problem.

When I glide back into the aisle, working my new little dance move, I'm getting excited about the possibility of a Strawberry Pop-Tart. Just then, who do I see?

Bailey James.

I sidle back into the cereal aisle, out of sight. But I can't help taking a second look.

It's him, all right. He's pushing a big blue cart, wearing an L.A. Lakers jersey. Walking beside a tall, stern-looking woman, who must be his mom. They're near Aisle 15, housewares, and she's looking at packages of place settings. She points to one, Bailey nods, and then she plops it into their cart.

Bailey wheels the cart around fast. I duck back, but not in time.

"Ella?" Bailey waves.

I can't go anywhere in this town.

Chapter 29

SMILING, I STEP OUT INTO THE AISLE. "HI, Bailey." I tuck the Pop-Tarts behind my back like some kind of contraband.

Bailey's mom is a tall, pretty woman with dark, smooth skin like my mom's. Her hair is straightened, pulled back in a bun. The lines of her face make her look very serious, but she smiles prettily when Bailey says, "Mom, this is Ella, my friend from school. She's the one with the basketball hoop."

Mrs. James nods at me. "Lovely to meet you, Ella."

"Hi, Mrs. James."

We stand in weird silence for a moment. Then Mrs. James relieves Bailey of the cart and says, "I'll meet you at the checkout, B." She gazes at him pointedly. "We cannot be late."

"Okay, Mom."

"Lakers fan?" I say when we're alone.

Bailey grins. I grin, relieved that he could tell I was joking.

"So," he says. "Sorry I don't have time to hang out."

"That's okay. Where are you going?"

Bailey shrugs. "Just this place we go," he says in a subject-changing kind of way. "I guess I'll see you tomorrow, then? Hoops?"

"Yeah, okay."

"Cool." Bailey holds out his fist, and I bump it. "See ya."

Then he's disappearing through the maze of aisles toward the checkout. I head back to automotive, clutching the holy Pop-Tarts. Thinking how easy it was, what just happened.

Bailey wants to be my friend. No, he called himself my friend. Maybe we even already *are* friends. Just like that. Easy.

It used to be easy all the time, having friends. Millie, Z, right next door. Now, Millie's off on her own, and Z's sitting amid a pile of tires waiting for things that aren't real to happen. Waiting for me to bring him Pop-Tarts so that the world will seem less tilted for a minute, when really we're all walking upside down.

Z holds out his hands, like a tray. I place a Pop-Tart on them, reverently.

"Yum," I say a second later, around a mouthful of my own Pop-Tart. "Don't let anyone tell you strawberry isn't the best flavor."

Z smiles, crumbs on his face, and nods. "Delicious, milady."

Two Pop-Tarts down, two to go.

Maybe I shouldn't have to work this hard. Maybe the things that are wrong don't get better when all you do is pretend.

"I ran into Bailey," I say, because I want to see what happens. "You know, from school? That's what took so long."

Z chews quietly for a while, his face a mask of moving parts. Then he licks Pop-Tart crumbs off his fingers and brushes some off his lap.

"The knight is white," he says, rotating the chessboard and making the first move.

Z pulls the special box back out and rests it in his lap. Except for that, that tiny-huge detail, he's acting like it's business as usual.

A flash of heat rushes my chest. Hot, stupid anger for no reason at all. "Aren't you going to say anything?"

"Milady?"

"I hung out with Bailey this week. You hate that. Just say it."

Z grabs the pawn he just moved and repositions it, like he's reminding me the game is already in progress.

"Your move, milady."

"Stop it. Why can't we just talk?" I say. "I know I hurt your feelings."

"Your move, milady." He's restless now, bouncing his knees and drumming the top of the Altoids box.

"I'm sorry, okay? I didn't mean for it to happen. Just say something real. Please."

Z covers his ears. His eyes are wide, his hands trembling. I think maybe he's going to cry or scream or fall over. But I can't make myself be nicer.

"Fine," I snap. "You don't care what I do. You're fine on your own."

He clutches the box and whispers, "It is natural for those with great power to find themselves alone."

"If that's what you want," I say. "You've got it."

Z stops moving altogether.

"I have to go find Grammie." I walk away, leaving him to his boxes, chessmen, and tires.

Chapter 30

WHEN WE GET HOME, I SHUT MYSELF in my room. It's bad, what I did. Yelling at Z. He doesn't mean to make things hard, he just . . . does.

It's not Z's fault. I don't know why I got so mad at him. I don't know what part of the body makes you get mad for no reason, but it feels like it comes from my belly. I don't know what part makes Z always want to pretend, but I'm guessing it's his brain, or his heart. The main parts of his engine.

I go to my bookshelf and pull out *The Body Book*. The clear, glossy pages flip back one by one, and you can see all the insides of the body. The skin, and everything underneath in there that makes people soft and squishy, right down to the bones that help us stand up straight. I like *The Body Book*.

Daddy gave it to me when he got sick. We looked at the pictures together so that I could understand. He told me the human body is like a machine. The brain and the heart are the main parts of the engine, and our lungs breathe air like gasoline to make us run.

The moral of the story was: Part of Daddy's engine was broken. His lungs.

"Grammie can fix that," I said. Now I know it's stupid, what I said. Daddy must have known it too, but he just laughed and kissed me hard on my head. "Grammie's good, but not that good," he whispered.

I let the pages of the book ripple down on top of each other, press the cover down.

I never did understand.

Chapter 31

THERE ARE LITTLE THINGS THAT HAPPEN. Little things that make a difference.

At breakfast Grammie drops a glass and it shatters on the kitchen floor. I stay to help her clean it up, which makes me late getting out of the house.

So I'm running, running for the bus. Millie stands in the open door, on the steps, making it wait for me. It's a little too much kindness from her this early in the morning. As we slump into our seats, I'm breathless and strangely on edge.

"Thanks."

Millie smiles, and suddenly I want to tell her everything. About Bailey and Z. I think she would understand.

"Why don't you braid your hair anymore?" is what comes out instead.

"What?" she says. "Sometimes I do."

This is falsehood. Untruth. Lie. I shake my head. "Never. Not since the first day of school."

I want to be mad at her. For leaving. For not looking back. But I also want to know how she did it, and if I can come, too.

"Well, I don't know," she says. "I can't wear my hair the same every day anymore. No one does that."

That stings. Especially because she knows that's exactly what I do. "Sure, yeah. What kind of loser would do that?" I reach up and yank the ribbons off the ends of my braids. My fingers itch to rip out my careful plaits, but luckily reason slips back into the mix. Jonathan Hoffman would have a field day if I showed up at school with a full, unruly 'fro.

"Ella . . ."

But I'm on a roll now. "And how come you stopped sitting with us at lunch?"

Millie gazes at me, puzzled. "You stopped sitting with me," she whispers. "You know you could sit with us anytime you want."

That's not how I remember it. One day it was the three of us together at a table with some other people. The next, it was me and Z. Alone.

"We can?" I say.

"Well, you can."

"Oh." There it is. The part I know deep down. The part I hate.

I can't do it to Z. Be a person who leaves. That's for everyone else. Not for us.

"It couldn't be the three of us forever." Millie looks out the window. "You chose him over me. And he's so *weird* now."

"You don't know anything about it," I snap. "How could you?"

"There's something wrong with him, Ella. Everyone knows it but you."

We climb off the bus, already not speaking. We climb off the bus into the strangest, most unexpected scene I could have imagined.

Chapter 32

A SMALL CROWD HAS GATHERED. IN THE center Bailey and Z circle each other as if they're going to throw down. I race toward them.

"Whoa, man," Bailey says. "Calm down."

Z shakes his fist at Bailey. I didn't think people really did that. I thought it was just an expression, but there he is, doing it.

"Return the treasure, you rogue," Z barks, his voice high and strained. Everyone laughs. Bailey seems bewildered.

"I don't know what you're talking about, man."

A few of the basketballers are egging Z on. Brandon and Miles mock him in the usual way, echoing his intense tone and odd phraseology.

"Yeah, you're such a rogue, Bailey," Brandon taunts.

"Go get your rogue on," cheers Miles.

The other guys clap and cheer as I weave through the circle. Then a strange thing happens where, for a moment, I'm just one of the crowd. I wasn't there when it started, standing by him. I don't know what happened. For the first time ever, I'm on the outside looking in. For the first time ever, I see how easy it would be to point and laugh along with everyone else. For the first time, I see how freakish and small we must look, going everywhere on our own, talking a different language. For the first time ever, for a very long moment, I hate us.

Z charges forth, oblivious, which only enhances their fun. "Return it at once!"

"Oooh, you're in trouble now," Brandon says gleefully.

"Back off," Bailey yells at them. "Leave him alone. Let me just figure this out."

By this point I've reached them. I rush up to Z. "What're you doing?" I whisper.

"Stand back, milady," he insists. He holds his chest out and raises his fists. "The return of the treasure is utmost. There may be bloodshed."

The others hoot and holler. Bailey puts out his arms, obviously confused. I fall back, a little scared of the expression on Z's face. He's flushed an angry red, and his knees are bent like he's going to spring. But he can barely maneuver under the weight of his backpack, and the picture he makes is beyond absurd.

He could never do any actual damage to Bailey, but what I don't understand is why he would want to. I return to his side.

"Stop it," I tell Z, pushing his fists down. "It's going to be okay." Then I round on Bailey. "What did you do? Why are you messing with him?"

Bailey puts up his hands, surrendering. "We were just hanging out. He came up on me all hot, talking about I stole his treasure."

"What did you take?"

"I'm telling you, nothing," Bailey says.

Z pounds his feet on the pavement, then stalks away to our corner. The others shout a few words after him but quickly lose interest. Thank goodness Jonathan Hoffman is nowhere in sight.

"What the—?" Bailey shakes his head. "That's one strange little dude."

"He's my friend," I snap. I have to do something, and fast, to make up for all the bad thoughts.

"I know—" Bailey crosses his arms and looks after Z. He's huddled at the corner of the building, digging into his backpack. "Does he have a problem with me?"

Well, of course he does. I like you, and he doesn't like that.

"Maybe. I don't know." I say as it dawns on me. Bailey did take something from Z, sort of. Z would see it that way. What Bailey took was . . .me.

I rub my forehead. Things just got way more complicated. "I have to go talk to him. We kind of got in a fight yesterday. I think this is my fault."

I walk away from Bailey, toward Z. When I get close, instead of turning toward me like usual, he gives me his back, hunching low over his bag and his boxes. With his arms, he shields it all from my view.

"Maybe he needs some space," Bailey says. He speaks right over my shoulder. He's followed me.

Bailey is the greatest boy ever. Right then and there, I realize it. He could be off with all his friends, making fun of the freak boy and the camo-faced girl and laughing, but instead he's here. He's trying to help. But I can't let him.

"We're fine." I push Bailey's arm gently. "Just go."

Bailey doesn't go. Instead he grabs my arm and pulls me a few yards away from where Z is working with his boxes, clearly lost in his own world.

"What's his deal?" Bailey says. "I'm just trying to understand what I did."

"No idea," I say, walking a little further away. "But he obviously doesn't want to see either of us right now."

"Just give him a day," Bailey says. "You can sit with us at lunch. Let him calm down."

"Maybe," I say. "Maybe at lunchtime."

"Hey, Ella." Bailey grins like he just remembered something. He reaches into his pocket. "Check it out." Bailey extends his hand. He's holding two round golden disks the size of large coins. They are stamped *Mirage* on one side, with neon palm trees and a big ten-dollar sign on the other.

"Casino chips?" I say.

"I found them on the grass," he says. "How cool is that? Twenty bucks, baby."

"Awesome," I say, trying to recall the last time I had twenty bucks in my hand. Unable to. "Can I touch them?"

Bailey turns them over into my palm. I've seen casino chips before. Grammie sometimes brings a few home from her Mondays in Vegas.

"You gonna keep them or cash them?"

"Kids aren't allowed in the casinos," he says. "How are we gonna turn it into money?"

"Oh, right."

"Maybe I'll keep 'em a while. For luck."

I nod. "A little luck never hurt anyone."

Bailey grins. "You want to hold one?"

"Really?"

"Don't say I never gave you anything." He plucks one from my hand but leaves the other. "Anyway, luck is luckiest when it's shared, right?"

I wonder where he heard that, or if he made it up.

The bell rings. Time to go to class. "Let's go inside," Bailey says, but I hang back.

"I'm going to wait a minute, okay?"

Bailey shrugs. "Catch you later," he says.

I look over my shoulder as Z gathers his boxes into his backpack and comes toward me. I wait because I know he'll come and that we'll walk inside together. Which he does, and we do. Like always.

There's something deep down that won't let me leave him. Like I know he's not going to be okay.

Chapter 33

Z AND I ARE STANDING IN THE HALLWAY BY our lockers. He hasn't uttered a word all morning, but I linger, hoping he'll change his mind and decide to speak to me again. I lean my shoulder against the lockers, waiting for him to finish dialing his combination, when suddenly someone's book bag slams me hard in the face. I'm startled into dropping my armful of books. My nose aches. My eyes start to tear. I blink, staggering backward, right into the wall. It knocks the wind out of me. The nose of a padlock digs hard into my spine.

I struggle to open my eyes, find myself staring into the face of the enemy.

"Watch where you're going, Camo-Face," Jonathan Hoffman says. Behind him Brandon and Miles are laughing.

His backpack dangles from his fingers. I know he did it on purpose.

Out of nowhere, Bailey appears. His body brushes past me, a blur. His fist flies, landing solidly in Jonathan Hoffman's face. The *thwack* practically echoes in the corridor. Jonathan cries out, a shocked, pathetic whimper. Then he narrows his eyes and throws a punch toward Bailey, who takes it on the chin.

Bailey dives at Jonathan. They roll and grunt, a thrashing mess of fists and elbows, muscles and knees. The sound of clothing tearing.

"Fight!" someone cries out, even though everyone in the hallway has already turned to look.

Bailey is bigger, stronger. He presses Jonathan down with his whole body, punching him. "Say it again," he gasps. "I dare you."

"Wh-what?" Jonathan stammers. His upper lip is bloody. It begins to smear his cheeks.

Bailey's face is hard. For a moment he looks so much older than all of us. Jonathan cowers on the floor, and I see how weak he is.

Mr. Pettigrew, our history teacher, pokes his head out of his classroom, then comes racing down the hallway. Another teacher wades through the crowd to take hold of Jonathan.

"All students to their classrooms. Now!" Mr. Pettigrew bellows. Kids scatter. I hang back, pressing against the lockers. Z is nowhere in sight.

My eyes water as I kneel down to gather my books and papers. I can't believe what I've just seen. I can't believe what happened.

I try to catch Bailey's eye as Mr. Pettigrew leads him and Jonathan past us down the hall toward the office. But he keeps his head down, his hand on his bruised jaw, and I decide it doesn't matter. My heart soars anyway. It soars because I can't believe he was fighting for me. That he threw himself between me and Jonathan, and for a second I didn't have to worry. When my tears start to blur his face again, I blink them away, because I want to see. I want to see my hero.

Chapter 34

CAN'T FOCUS ON ANYTHING NEXT PERIOD. ALL that matters is what Bailey did. How everyone knows now that he's on my side. Bailey and Ella. Ella and Bailey. Us. We. E+B=4EVR.

My seat is near the classroom window. I see Mrs. James arrive, wearing an office-looking outfit, clicking the car locked as she hurries toward the school. Shortly after, she's back, with Bailey.

I watch as they walk through the parking lot. She's shaking her head and talking fast. He holds his head down. Then she hugs him and puts him in the car.

The Mirage casino chip finds its way into my palm and rests there.

"Don't say I never gave you anything." As if he hadn't already given enough.

Chapter 35

EVERYONE'S TALKING ABOUT THE FIGHT. I weave through the crowd toward the lunch line. Bailey's name is on everyone's lips. I don't hear my name anywhere yet, but that doesn't matter. Everyone saw. Everyone knows. Today, thanks to Bailey, maybe it'll be okay to sit somewhere new. At least until Z comes around.

I carry my tray toward Millie's table. I refuse to feel bad about it. Z doesn't want much to do with me today, anyway. He made that perfectly clear this morning. And Millie and Bailey both said I could.

"Hi, Ella," Cass says as I approach. "There's plenty of room." I slide my tray down. Could it really be this simple?

At the guys' end of the table, the conversation is going strong, still about the fight.

"How'd it even start?" Kurt says. I hold my breath.

"Jonathan majorly dissed the army," Max says. He sighs. "Right in front of Bailey. Total punk move."

"Yeah," Rick agrees.

My heart sinks low. That's not how it happened. Is it? Or what if it is? What if it wasn't about them calling me names? What if what Bailey hates is Jonathan talking down camo— an army thing. Maybe he doesn't care at all about me.

"His dad's a war hero, you know," Rick says. "Hoffman didn't stand a chance."

"Yeah, yeah," Max says. "His dad got some big medal for saving this whole platoon of soldiers who were marooned between a bunch of enemy tanks. And another time, he fought his way out of an Iraqi prison with one pistol and only two bullets."

Max glows on about Bailey's dad's escapades. "He taught Bailey everything he knows, so it totally makes sense that he would, like, dominate. Jonathan just didn't know what he was messing with."

I pick at the lump of gray-brown casserole on my tray. For a guy who doesn't like to talk about it, everyone sure seems to know a lot about Bailey's dad.

Millie chooses that moment to arrive, plunking her tray next to mine with a cheerful "Hey, Ella." As if all is forgotten because, for once, I've chosen her.

But I haven't. This was just a trial run, and a Big Fat Failure at that. I grab my tray and jump up, fleeing the scene.

I land beside Z, who steadfastly refuses to return my gaze.

In time, things will go back to normal. Right? I'll find a way to let Z know that I'm done with trying to be things I'm not. I'm a little bit Ella and a little bit Eleanor, and that'll be just fine for now, thank you.

The casino chip still buried deep in my palm begins to ache. I flatten my hand so it falls, tiny, on the tabletop.

Z cuts his eyes toward me, toward the chip, actually. "It's not special," he says dully. "There are many more where that came from."

I push my tray toward him and lay my head on the table. It's all I can do not to die on the spot.

Chapter 36

IT'S A LONG WALK HOME AFTER THAT. A LONG, SLOW walk. Alone.

For a minute there, things were almost going great. Everything was about to change. I wanted it to so bad. So bad I messed things up with Z. All for Bailey, when none of what happened was really how I thought it was.

I'm so stupid. How could I think for one second that I had anything in common with someone like him? He's Bailey James. Basketball Star. Hero. King of the Popular Table. And who am I?

Plain old Ella.

Camo-Face.

Friend to freaks and losers.

I squeeze my backpack straps with tight fists.

This is why I need Eleanor. This is why I need Z. For all the moments when the rest of the world turns as ugly as I am and it gets hard to manage it.

How could I forget that? How could I believe things could ever be another way?

Because of Bailey, that's why.

Who does Bailey James think he is, coming in and acting all friendly when, really, he's just one of *them*? Why'd he have to mess with me? Things weren't perfect around here, but it was nothing I couldn't handle. Why'd he have to come in and show me how different things could be? Why couldn't he have just left well enough alone?

I swing my leg hard, as if there was anything there to be kicked. Throw up my fists and fight with the air for a minute. How did it feel, I wonder, when Bailey put his fist in Jonathan Hoffman's face? It had to feel great. Only now, it's Bailey who I hate. It's Bailey whose face I want to put my fist in. Bring on all his war hero moves. Whatever he's got. Why did he have to lie? I hate him.

Back in my own yard, I run to the basketball hoop. I grab hold of the metal pole, pushing, tugging, wondering how hard it'd be to pull it out, but it's in deep. It doesn't move a bit. I rest my head against it.

He fooled me and I fell for it. He had me believing—

It doesn't matter. It's over now.

Before, I felt left out. Alone. But that was before I met Bailey, when I had no idea what I was really missing. Now? Now the usual just isn't good enough anymore.

Chapter 37

CARRY THE BASKETBALL UNDER MY ARM AS I WALK down the street toward Bailey's house. I'll give it back, and that'll be that. It was never going to work out, me and him being friends. It's better this way.

I try to stay mad at him, but it's hard. The mad starts to fade into sad. Whatever else Bailey is—liar, popular boy, ultimate fighting machine—he's also the kind of boy who doesn't make fun of Z and who will maybe possibly get in a fight over you. Deep down, I still think that's what happened—and it's not easy to be mad at that. Plus, we had fun together. Maybe he was just messing with me the whole time, but I don't really think so.

Anyway, it's over now. I'll return the ball and say I'm sorry for getting him into a mess. And I also want to know why, if we are supposed to be friends, he will tell everyone in the world about his dad, except me. I thought we knew each other. I thought we had this thing in common. I want to look at him and say, Did you ever really want to be friends, or did you just want to use my basketball hoop?

I ring the bell.

Bailey's mom answers the door.

"Hi," I say.

Mrs. James gazes upon me, kindly enough. "I'm sorry, Ella. Bailey's grounded today."

"Oh."

She smiles apologetically and starts to close the door.

"It's my fault," I blurt. "Don't make him in trouble."

Mrs. James studies me for a moment. Then she steps out of the doorway. "Come inside."

Bailey's house is unfinished. That's what I think when I look around. I step into a wide foyer that opens into the dining area and the living room. There's furniture that looks cozy, pictures on the walls, and knickknacks on the tables, but everything still somehow looks bare. In the dining room there's a tall pile of moving boxes and a square folding table with two chairs.

"Where's Bailey?"

Mrs. James shakes her head. "He's in his room. Grounded, remember?"

"Oh."

"I'm steeping some tea," she says. I stare at her. She smiles. "We also have juice."

"Juice, please."

I stand awkwardly in the hallway while she melts through the dining area into the kitchen. The soft clatter of dishes reaches me. I'm quickly losing the nerve to say the things I wanted to say. If Bailey came out from around a corner right now, I think all I would have to say out loud is hello.

A column of framed photographs hangs on the wall. I drift toward it, curious. Three photos that tell a story. At the top, a man and a woman. Bailey's mom. She looks young and calm and pretty, hugging the man in his military dress uniform while he leans in to kiss her cheek. The man has a friendly face, not handsome, but not ugly. Bailey's dad. The war hero.

Below that, the couple with a small boy: Bailey, several years ago. He's dressed in a miniature suit, clutching the staff of a small American flag. His dad, dressed in desert combat fatigues, has him held up close in his arms.

At the bottom, the mom and the boy, older, all alone.

"Juice," Mrs. James reports from behind me. I whip around, caught in the act of looking too close.

"How did he die?" I blurt.

A horrible, wrong question. "Never mind. I'm sorry."

I wave my hand, trying to rub it away. "I'm sorry."

Mrs. James hands me the cup of juice and motions for me to follow her. We settle onto the couch in the living room.

"Did Bailey tell you his father died?" she says softly.

I nod, then think about it. "N-no. I guess not. But—"

"Okay." She lets out a little breath. She seems relieved.

I know he's somewhere close by, behind a thin wall, but I've never felt further from Bailey. I sip juice from my cup. And out of nowhere I'm trying not to cry.

"Bailey talks about you a lot," Mrs. James says. "That's why I thought we should sit down, so I could meet his new friend."

Bailey talks about me? "He has lots of friends," I say. "Everyone's his friend."

Mrs. James smiles. "Hmmm." She sips her tea thoughtfully.

I have to get something off my chest. "He got in the fight because of me."

"Oh?"

"He was protecting me." My knight in shining armor, I almost say. But I trip over the words because he can't be my knight. Z is. Bailey has to be something else. "He's really brave. Like his dad, right?"

Mrs. James sits, listening, so I go on.

"Jonathan said something mean to me. He's just really mean," I blurt. "I'm glad Bailey hit him. He deserved it."

"What did he say?"

I sit quietly. It echoes in my head, but I don't like to say it out loud.

"Well, I suppose it doesn't matter," Mrs. James says after a moment.

I sip my juice. "Is he still grounded?"

"Oh, yes, ma'am."

"But—"

"You can't make someone fight, Ella. It's not your fault. And he has to learn to solve problems another way."

"It was just one time," I say.

Mrs. James sips her tea.

I don't know much, but I know that when grown-ups sit quietly, it means there's a secret in the room. It means you're a child and there are things you're not supposed to know. Sometimes you know them anyway. Like how I know when Mom is missing Dad, or when Grammie's worried about money, or when the teachers think Z's all screwed up. Like how I knew something horrible was happening when Dad got sick, even before anyone told me. Before Dad showed me *The Body Book* and tried to explain.

I don't know what all is in the room with us now. Maybe I don't want to know.

I set my juice cup on the coffee table. "I have to go home now."

"Of course." Mrs. James settles her teacup in the saucer.

"Will you tell Bailey . . ." I pause. I roll the basketball off my lap and onto the sofa where I was just sitting. I wait as it settles in the cushion crack.

It's better this way. I want to go back to the way things were. With Z, I never have to wonder where I stand. I never have to wonder what's real and what's not.

"Tell him he can still use the hoop if he wants."

Chapter 38

THE FRONT DOOR SLAMS A LITTLE TOO HARD on my way into the house, but I try to slip away to my room, unnoticed. That, or my stomping footsteps, gives me away.

"Just one second there, sparky," Grammie calls, motioning me back. "What's this face?"

"That's just how I look," I mutter. "I'm ugly."

"Nonsense," Grammie declares. "I don't want to hear that kind of talk out of you, missy."

I touch my cheeks in despair. "Well, it's true whether I say it or not, so what's the difference?"

"Come over here."

My feet stay planted, far away. I want to fight Grammie's sharp tone, fight the words that try to fix it when we know it can't ever be fixed. So she springs toward me, the Energizer Bunny of unhelpfulness.

"This is a beautiful face," she says, her fingers flitting over the surface of me.

"Ugly," I insist.

"Nope. One day you're gonna see it. I promise." She kisses my forehead.

"We're not supposed to lie to each other," I say. That's one of the rules around here.

Grammie clucks her tongue at me. "Anyone who can see will see you beautiful," she says, which is what they always say. She slides her fingers into my knots of curl.

It's not Grammie's fault. Grandmas are supposed to think you're beautiful. They have to, because it's their job, and also because if they didn't love you as hard as they could, you might just die of ugliness.

"Oh, no you don't." Grammie reaches out and clutches me to stop me from running past. "Come into my arms, cuddlebug."

She folds me up against her, and I let her. I squeeze my eyes shut. Sometimes, for just a second, I find a way to believe her. But it never lasts.

"Now then, what's the real trouble here?" She sets me back and studies me.

"There's this boy."

"Ah." Grammie gazes upon me wisely.

I shouldn't have brought it up. "Just don't say anything, okay?" I close my eyes.

Grammie goes, "Humph." Which in this case means, *Child, how long have you known me?*

All the breath and the fight go out of me. "Okay, let's have it."

"I lived a whole long life," Grammie says. "Only one man I found worth giving the time of day." She touches the locket that Grampa must've given her.

"Hey," I say, lifting my head. "What about Daddy?"

Grammie waves her hand. "Oh, he doesn't count for me. That's my baby."

"Tomorrow —," I say, so she knows I didn't forget.

"That's right," Grammie says. She opens up her locket so we can see the tiny pictures of Daddy and me. "It's three years tomorrow."

Chapter 39

WAKE IN THE MORNING AND TURN TO MY NIGHT-stand, gazing at the framed photo smiling back at me. I know what he's trying to tell me. Today is a day to be brave. Today is a day to not close my eyes.

Sorry, Daddy.

I make my way through the bathroom the way I always do. Something should be different about Dad's day, I think, but for some reason I can't let it be that. The radio's playing quietly when I come down the hallway. Grammie stands in her socks in the kitchen, sipping coffee from her big blue mug. I hug her around the middle.

"Goodness knows, you're getting tall," she murmurs. It's true. My head reaches her shoulder, and I can look over without standing on tiptoe. I lean my head against her anyway.

Grammie smooths back my braids, then smacks me lightly on the hip. "It's just a regular day, kiddo. Up and at 'em."

It's not a regular day, but it sure looks like one. I ride the bus beside Millie, who sits in stony silence for two minutes before informing me that she's thinking of going with Max instead of Rick, and what do I think.

When we get off, Z waits at the corner of the school, two cheese biscuits in hand. He gives me one. I wonder what sort of place he's found in his world for our fight. How he's able to make sense of it and let it wash away.

I tear the biscuit in half and give part back to him. "You eat it, okay?" I haven't been very good to him lately, and maybe I owe him a little more kindness. He munches happily, and I sit beside him, watching the other kids in their groups. We're comfortable. Apart. Like usual.

The first bell rings, and we go inside. At the lockers, Z digs around in his bag for an extra long time. We're about to go our separate ways, finally, when I feel his little hand on my backpack. I'm wearing it on both shoulders, so I don't see what the problem is. I keep walking.

"Milady," he murmurs.

I turn, even though at this rate we're going to be late for class. "Z—"

He holds out his palm. In it rests a little wooden heart, painted pale blue, with the number three on it.

This is the kind of thing he does just right. Just right enough to break my heart.

"You remembered."

Z tilts his head, stares into the near distance. I wonder what he's thinking, or if this is just a little too close to real for him to come all the way with me.

"Thanks," I whisper. I grab the tiny token off his hand and hurry toward the classroom.

Chapter 40

SCHOOL FEELS EMPTY WITHOUT BAILEY. I'M sure he's in the building, in the in-school suspension classroom with Jonathan, but I can't catch a glimpse of him. Everyone's done talking about the fight, so it's like he never even existed. Business as usual. Almost.

The Mirage casino chip still in my pocket reminds me that he was real. Is real. That he'll be back, with his basketball jerseys and his giant grin and trying to win me over. Or maybe he can take a hint. Maybe it's all already over.

"Can I borrow a dollar?" Cass says to Millie on the way to the cafeteria. "My mom gave me lunch money this morning, but I can't find it now."

A second later this guy Brad starts complaining that the

five dollars that were in his pocket before gym class weren't there after.

"It's an epidemic," Max says. "Brandon's cash disappeared, too."

People's lunch money is missing. That's the topic of conversation today. I hear them talking, but I also kind of float above it, thinking of Bailey while trying not to step on Z's heels. He moves at a stalking pace in front of me.

In my other pocket rests the little blue heart he gave me. This is one of those times when I just don't understand him. Remembering the anniversary is about as real as it gets, but he finds a way to go there. Although he won't say an actual word about it. It's like the fantasy is heightened, or something. But he does know what's happening.

All around, Z is in rare form today. Maybe it's the lack of Bailey, I don't know, but he cannot stop talking all through lunch. He's high on something—some tidbit of fantasy, or just having me all to himself again. Sort of. To be honest, I'm not really listening.

"The quest begins today, milady," Z says.

"What?" I say for the thousandth time this morning.

"The quest," Z insists. "It's a long journey, but in the city of gold we will find the treasure," he chirps.

Just then, I see him. Bailey. From a distance, going

through the lunch line after everyone else has finished. I sit up straighter.

Z chatters on and on about his adventure, his quest. This is something new. I don't get it yet. Eventually I'll figure it out and be able to play along.

Bailey's already headed for the door, trailing Jonathan. Both look extremely bummed out over their current lot in life. The ISS teacher nudges them to keep moving. They're not allowed to talk to anyone.

At the last possible second, Bailey turns his head. Looks at me, sees me looking back. His expression is flat, full of nothing. He stares for one second, then slinks out the door. I don't know what it means.

Chapter 41

WHEN THE LAST BELL RINGS, Z IS nowhere to be found. I wait by his locker for a minute, but when he doesn't appear, I figure maybe he already knows it's a no chess kind of day. I go ahead outside and, sure enough, Mom's waiting in the pickup line.

It's Dad's day, so she drives us straight to the Unitarian church. There's no service going on, but the doors are open, so we sit in the back pew. We fold our hands and bow our heads to say a prayer of thanks for his life. It's okay to cry a little, so Mom does, but I don't feel like it today, so I just lean my head on her shoulder. Who knows what you're supposed to say in a prayer, so I ask the angels to give him good wings and fresh batteries for his halo so it will shine nice and bright.

Last year we wore a lot of black, went to the Catholic church, and lit candles. The year before that, Dad's day actually fell on a Sunday, so we got to do a whole big worship service with the Baptists, who sing a lot. We were at the church all day, because we figured out that saying "Lord Jesus, amen" is like a form of currency that can buy you things like hugs and fried chicken with a side of coleslaw. We don't really fit in any of these places, but Mom says it's the least we can do in memory of Dad and that it doesn't hurt to spread it around.

Mom keeps tissues in her purse, and now her face is running like a faucet, so I dig around until I find some that seem unused. She accepts them with one of those teary smiles that is supposed to say a bunch of things at once, things like *I'm sad and it's okay,* but also *I wish you didn't have to see me like this,* and *Don't worry, I'm really happy underneath, even though I don't look it.*

I lean against her again and try to pray something different. I want the angels to look out for Mom, too. Dad being gone, well, I don't think about that too much because it's sometimes hard to remember when he wasn't. Mom being gone, though. I think about that a lot when she's away. A few days at a time is bad enough. I can't imagine it being forever.

She knows what I'm thinking, I guess, because she

slides her arm around me from the side and hugs me closer. "Love, and stuff," she whispers in my ear. "Love, love, love."

On the way home, Mom's still a little sniffly. I don't like it when she cries, but Grammie always says if you feel like crying, you should just go ahead, and there's no shame in it. So I can't really ask her to stop.

"Oh, I miss Daddy," Mom says, blotting her face. "I miss him a little bit every day."

She glances at me, and I think I'm supposed to say something, but I don't.

Instead, I stare out the window. I miss Daddy. I do. I have the picture of him on my nightstand that I look at every morning and every night. But when I don't look right at it, sometimes it's hard to picture his face. Some days I come home from school, and I see the picture, and I realize I forgot to miss him. Usually it's because I was too busy being mad at Jonathan or worried about what he was going to do to me or to Z. Or because we had a really good chess game. Or, lately, because of Bailey.

Speak of the devil.

Mom pauses the car in the street, because Bailey's in the driveway. We watch for a moment as he loops the ball high a few times before he sees us. He waits in the grass by the pole while we pull into the garage.

Mom puts her hand on my thigh. "What do you want to do?" she says. I suppose she means about Bailey.

"This is what we do after school," I say, leaping out of the car before she can follow me with more words.

Chapter 42

EY," I SAY.

"Hey," he says. He bounces the ball slowly, such that when it returns after each drop it seems to hang in the air. His fingers barely skim it, guiding it down. Graceful. Sad.

"Hey," I say again. I'm glad he's here, but I don't know what to do with him.

I push up my sleeves.

"Thought you didn't want to play with me anymore." Bailey bounces the ball in a wide, slow V between his two hands. He looks like some kind of strange bird, raising one wing at a time.

"After the fight," I say, "Max was telling everybody about all the combat moves your dad taught you."

Bailey dribbles fast, glances at me. He passes the ball to

himself over my head, racing around to receive it. "Yeah."

"And all these other stories . . . ," I trail off.

Bailey dribbles through the silence.

"How come you didn't tell me?" I say.

Dribble. Spin. Dribble. "It's no big thing."

"Yeah, huh." I cross my arms.

Dribble. Dribble. Shoot.

"Well . . . ?" I say.

"So, he's a war hero. So what?" Bailey snaps. "Maybe I still don't like to talk about it."

"Then how come everybody knows?" I snap back.

"The guys at school," he says. "They're all into that kind of stuff. So I just—" He waves his hand. "It's easier."

Bailey grins, dribbles the ball, glances up at the basket, so natural. So easy.

Then I see it. His perfect, smiling expression cracks. It's only for a second, but his face splits into something so familiar, so broken. I find myself looking harder.

"Can we just play now?" he says. He cups the ball at his chest, ready to send it my way.

"Wait—," I blurt.

He doesn't. The ball comes at me fast. My hands go up to stop it, but I'm not that good. It smacks my palms and bounces away.

Bailey hops to retrieve it, dribbles, shoots. But he's

looking at me as the ball swoops through the net. When it bounces this time, I'm close enough to catch it. This time I'm ready.

For a second I just hold it in my hands, feeling its skin. That little bit of roughness.

"C'mon, pass it."

Bailey's eyes meet mine. "If you just play really hard," he says, "nothing else matters."

Chapter 43

I THINK I KNOW WHAT BAILEY'S TALKING ABOUT. We run and jump and wipe sweat off our faces, and it's like the rest of the world fades away.

It's all ball, and air, and net, and Bailey. Hands, and shots, and shoes, and jumps. Grinning, counting, dribbling, laughing. The time just goes by. After a while I begin to see what Bailey must see in basketball. It's not just a game. It's not just fun. It's another way to pretend things are different. If you just play really hard, nothing else matters. And I love it.

Problem is, there's no hiding forever.

"Who's that?" Bailey says. Our game is suspended. I look up to see a short, thin, blond woman leaping out of the passenger seat of a car. The car drives off, and she rushes up our driveway. She hurries toward me, frantic.

"Is he here, Ella? Please tell me he's here," she blurts.

It's Z's mom.

Chapter 44

"WELL, DID YOU CHECK THE LIBRARY? He goes there every day." I try to act like things are fine, but I know deep down something's wrong. I stand in my living room, staring at Mom and Lynn, sitting side by side on the couch.

"The quest begins, milady." I didn't know what it meant. I didn't understand. I wasn't listening.

Up until a minute ago Lynn was in full panic mode. I told Bailey he had to go; then I brought her straight inside to see Mom. Mom knows how to calm people down.

Lynn seems better now, but I think she's passed the not-calm onto me. My stomach hurts.

"Yes," Lynn says. "The library and school. I was hoping—" She swallows hard. "If he's not here, then I'm at a loss."

"Well, then, he must be at Walmart," I say. *"The quest begins, milady."* Where did he go?

Lynn shakes her head. "He's not."

"Of course he is."

"We paged him throughout the store. Everyone who was on shift helped look."

Lynn glances at me. I can tell she's nervous that I'll say something I shouldn't. It's a secret that they live in the store. One of the things I'm not supposed to know.

"He's small," I say. "He likes to hide." I list some places we've found him before: in the laundry machines, under the shelves, on the shelf pretending to be a piece of merchandise, behind other merchandise. Once he climbed inside a column of tire rims and couldn't get back out. As I'm talking, Mom gazes at me with an expression I don't quite recognize.

"If he's spying, you have to call him Agent Z or he won't come out, remember?"

Lynn shakes her head. "It's a gut feeling," she says, holding a fist to her stomach. "He's not there."

"Lynn," Mom says. "How long has this been going on?"

"He's fine," Lynn says with a tight smile. "He's just so creative. He gets carried away. It's all a game to him."

Mom's wearing one of her super-grown-up looks now. The kind that means run for your life. I edge toward the doorway.

"It sounds a little more serious than that," Mom says, laying her hand on Lynn's back. At the same time she pins a Look on me that says, *Where do you think you're going, missy?* and crooks her finger at me. Against my better judgment, I go over there.

"No, no. Everything's fine," Lynn insists. "It's been so hard for him, since we . . . moved. Excuse me." Lynn jumps up and hurries into the bathroom.

When we're alone, Mom brushes the sides of my head with her fingers. "Honey," she says. "Why didn't you tell me what's been going on?"

"What's been going on?" I say. Because it's not going to be me who rats out Z and his mom.

Mom gives me a pointed look. "Don't play dumb."

"Z's just being Z," I say.

"Z?" Mom says, her eyebrows raised. "What is Z? You're calling him Agent Z?"

That's right. Mom only knows him by his real name, but that's not him anymore. And it's why I shouldn't say anything more.

"No. Well, that's what he wants. . . . Never mind," I say. "It's a long story."

I'm not good at lying. I'm not good at the truth. So it's best not to say anything at all.

"Where is he, Ella?" Mom says.

I shake my head. "I'm sure he's in the store. Or the library." But I'm not sure. There's something more, there's something else. If he's not there, he's somewhere, and I'm the one who should know where. *"The quest begins today, milady."*

Mom studies me, maybe upset, maybe disappointed. I don't know, but I don't like it. "Truth," she says softly, just as the bathroom door opens. "Do you know where he is?"

I'm scared now. Because I really don't.

Chapter 45

OM OFFERS TO DRIVE LYNN TO THE police station so she can report Z missing. I can't believe he's really missing, but in the bottom of my stomach, I know he's gone someplace.

Out the window, I watch the car pull out of the garage and take off down the street. Bailey's sitting on the front porch step, staring into space.

"What are you still doing here?" I snap. He pivots around to look at me. Something about the way he is right now makes me think I should've just let him come in before.

"What do you want?" I say. "Z's missing. He might have run away." As the words cross my lips, they don't feel right. To Z, it wouldn't be running away. To Z, it would be a grand adventure, something with meaning, something with weight. There would be a reason. What was his mission? Where would he go?

"Yeah, I picked up on that."

I cross my arms. I can barely contain the scared feeling. Z's out there somewhere, alone. He shouldn't be alone.

"I think I know where to look," Bailey says.

"What?" There's no way he can know. No way to get inside Z's head. If I can't, no one can. "No, you don't."

"I have an idea," he says. "From something he said the other day."

"Forget about it," I say. "Wherever he is, he's fine. He's just . . . he plays games. He'll be fine."

The way Bailey looks at me then, I know he can see through me. I'm not a great liar, but it's not about that. Whatever the stuff is that he won't talk about is still there, in the air. It reaches out and finds the same thing in me. His voice is soft. "Yeah, 'cause you're not at all worried."

Bailey James. Somehow he knows how to rip my heart wide open. I almost feel like I could tell him everything. But I can't tell him the truth about Z. Maybe Bailey is a good secret keeper, but they aren't my secrets to tell.

"You don't know me," I say. "You don't know us."

Bailey shrugs. "It was just an idea." He rolls the basketball against the porch with his palm pressed over it.

"Okay, fine. Where is he?" I hug my arms tighter. I tap my toe.

Bailey reaches into his pocket. He flicks his wrist and a small item comes sailing through the air toward me.

My hands fly up to catch it. My fingers slide along the chip's smooth edges.

"What?" I turn the chip over. Its neon palm trees and bold black stamp scream at me. Still, it takes me a moment to get Bailey's point. "You think he went to The Mirage? But that's on the Strip," I say. "In Vegas."

"I've been thinking about it," Bailey says. "He wigged out when he saw the chip."

"He did not 'wig out,'" I snap.

"Yeah," Bailey says. "He's weird to begin with, and that's cool"—he raises his hands to ward off my protest—"but when he saw me with the chip, he went a little postal."

"Why would he care about a stupid chip?" But I'm remembering the look on his face when I laid it on the table.

"There are many more where that came from." Z's words float back to me, from somewhere. I thought he was being matter-of-fact. Trying to put Bailey's gift down, in a small way.

"He would never go all the way to Vegas. Not by himself."

"It's not that far," Bailey says. "Not even half an hour on the bus."

"I know," I say. "But still." It's on the tip of my tongue to say that he not only wouldn't, he couldn't. To get on a bus and ride all the way into the city would have to bring him pretty close to reality at some point. I don't know how he could make it fit into his fantasy. But, then, Z's magic was that he could make anything fit. Absolutely anything.

My hand begins to ache. My fist is clenched around the chip, and it's leaving indentations in my palm. I relax.

"Well?" Bailey says.

"I don't know. Maybe." It was a theory. And heaven knows, I didn't have one of my own.

A thought crystallizes in my brain. Z saw Bailey with the chip. Bailey gave me the chip. Z saw me with the chip and knew where I got it. *There are many more where that came from.* What if he went to the casino hoping to get a chip to give me? Maybe he thought if he could deliver, I would forget about Bailey once and for all.

"It's my fault," I murmur. I turned my back on Z, and he panicked.

"Naw," Bailey says with a frown. "It's way bigger than that."

And maybe it is. *There are many more where that came from.* Bailey's chips are ten-dollar chips. If Z understands that chips equal money . . . well, he needs money.

Bailey says something else, but I ignore him. I'm already

keklamagoon

running into the house. I make straight for the kitchen cabinet where Grammie keeps her wad of cash. I tug four ten-dollar bills out from under the rubber bands, vowing that I'll pay her back out of my allowance, even if it takes all year.

I move fast. Bailey's just in the doorway when I'm back. He holds the screen open as I go streaking past.

"You okay, Ella?" Bailey chases me down the driveway.

"I have to go find him," I blurt. "Right now, before he does anything he shouldn't."

Chapter 46

I JOG DOWN THE STREET, HEADED INTO TOWN. BY the time I round the corner, Bailey hasn't dropped back, although his house is in the other direction.

"What are you doing?" I pant.

"Well, obviously, I'm coming with you."

"What?" I stop running. I'm out of breath, anyway. "You get that I'm going to Vegas, right?"

"Yeah, sure." Bailey shrugs. "I'm grounded, anyway. It's not like I have anything better to do."

My eyes narrow. "Oh, yeah. What are you doing out in the first place?"

Bailey grins mischievously. "My mom's still at work."

I shake my head. "Go home, then. We won't be back in time."

"Whatever," Bailey says. "I can't let you go alone. This is way too awesome."

Not the word I'd use to describe it. But to be honest, I don't want to go alone. And I want to stand here arguing with Bailey even less. "Well, come on, then."

We hurry toward town. The public buses run to and from Las Vegas every so often, but I don't know the schedules and I'm not about to miss a bus by mere minutes.

"We're good," Bailey says, pointing at the departures board. "Carson City is leaving now, but the five thirty-five to Vegas leaves in ten minutes.

"Give me the cash," he adds. "I'll buy us tickets." The forty bucks are clenched in my now-sweaty fist. I hand him twenty.

"Great. Stay out here for a minute," he says, peeking in the bus depot window. "And stay out of sight. I don't think they're supposed to let kids buy bus tickets."

My hopes fall flat. I hadn't thought of that. At all. "Oh. So it's hopeless."

"No, no. Let me work my magic," he says, slipping through the bus station door.

I squeeze one eye up against the window, peering through a narrow space between the edge of the wall and a sun-bleached poster inviting me to join the National Guard.

When it's Bailey's turn at the window, I hold my breath. After several long moments of talking and a few wild hand gestures by Bailey, the clerk reluctantly stamps two tickets and hands him his change.

Bailey emerges grinning triumphantly. He waves two tickets in my face. I'm duly impressed, but curious.

"So, how'd you do it?"

Bailey shrugs. "You really don't want to know the details," he says. "There's such a thing as plausible deniability."

"There's such a thing as *what*?"

"It means if anyone asks you later, you can say you don't know how I got them, and you'll be telling the truth." He hands me my seven dollars change.

I pocket the cash. We'll need it later, when it's time to come back. "I want to know."

"Trust me, you don't," Bailey says. He won't meet my eye when he says it.

I glance up at the big wall clock above the station's front door. There are five minutes between now and when the bus leaves, and I intend to spend them getting information out of Bailey.

What would I have done? "Did you lie and say the other ticket was for your mom or something?"

Bailey glances at me. "Yeah. I started with that. But I had to go bigger."

A bus pulls into the lot. A voice over a not-very-loud loudspeaker squawks, "That'll be the five thirty-five to Las Vegas. All aboard!"

"Let's go," Bailey says.

A couple of people disembark. The driver tears our tickets along with the others without giving us much of a glance. We climb up and slide into a pair of seats about halfway back. Across the aisle a man reading a newspaper peers over his glasses at us, then beyond us, then back.

"You kids traveling alone?"

"No, sir," Bailey says, leaning across me from the window seat. "I don't think they'd allow that."

"What about you?" I pipe in, hoping to change the subject. I'm suddenly wishing we'd chosen a seat further back. More isolated. The bus isn't empty, but it's not packed, either. "What brings you to Las Vegas?"

"Oh, I like to try my luck every few months," he says. He chuckles. "Ain't got much of it, though."

Bailey and I laugh too. "Well, good luck to you," Bailey says. There's a tone in his voice that says *Nice talking to you, but we're done now*. I couldn't have managed it.

The man nods and goes back to reading his paper. The bus starts moving, and Bailey and I both stare out the window as if we're fascinated by the desert landscape.

As the town rolls by and quickly gives way to scrub

brush and open sky, the hugeness of what we're doing hits me. Getting this far was fun, almost like a game. Now it gets real. My stomach sinks.

We're going to be in so much trouble.

Chapter 47

I'S A TWENTY-MINUTE RIDE, BUT HALFWAY THROUGH it feels like a hundred hours have passed. Miles of desert whip by the windows as my level of dread blossoms. Did it get this real for Z, when the bus doors closed and the engine rumbled? Was he able to imagine his trusty steed stamping and pawing beneath him, or did he panic? I'm scared for him, out here all on his own. At least I have Bailey.

We took a long car trip to California one time. It was after Daddy got sick, because he wanted to see the ocean again. We drove all day and all night, then had a picnic in the sand and danced in the waves for hours before it was time to come home. I remember the ocean, but the best part was all the car riding. I looked out the window and wondered what would happen if we never turned the car around but just kept going and going. Where would we end up? What would we see? Could we just drive forever? The three of us, frozen in time, frozen in motion, locked in a space where nothing would ever change.

The same fleeting thought crosses my mind now — what if I never went back? What would it be like to pick up and start over in a new place where no one knows me? No Jonathan Hoffman, no Millie . . . no Z. Maybe I could bring Bailey, though. We could go live in Las Vegas, where casino chips would flow in the imported water fountains, and we would never need anything more than that. Would we be happy? Would people learn to look away, to leave us alone? Is the world full of Jonathan Hoffmans, or is there something better out there?

I nudge Bailey's arm.

"You lived a lot of places," I say. "Where is best?"

"I don't know," Bailey murmurs. "I don't remember everywhere." He seems a bit distracted.

"Well, the stuff you don't remember can't be any good. Where was good?" Who knows, after this day is over, we may have to go on the lam. Mom is going to kill me, and I'm guessing Bailey's mom is probably going to do the same.

"Huh?" Bailey stares out the window, not really listening. After a moment he touches his fingers to the glass.

A high fence runs along the sides of the highway. Miles of nothing, and then a fence?

The fence is blocking off a piece of land, with a large building situated on it, well away from the road. So far back, in fact, that it's hard to even tell what kind of building it is, besides large and gray-white, and very secure with barbed wire atop all the fences.

"What is that place?" I wonder.

The man across the aisle glances up from his newspaper.

"It's a hospital," he says. "For soldiers."

Bailey drops his hand away. Fast.

My mind closes around something. One of the unspoken things. "Oh, no."

"Yep," the man says as if I'm talking to him. He takes off his glasses and dangles them by one stalk. "Not a regular VA, though. This is for the ones that are sick in the head. Wacko."

Bailey tenses up beside me, whips his head around.

"Some of them come back pretty messed up." The man taps his temple and shrugs. "No wonder, after the things they seen. Done. Who wouldn't go a little nuts?"

"Shut up!" Bailey shouts. "You don't know!" He leans over me, the glow of rage making him seem bigger than normal. I think if I wasn't sitting there, blocking him in, he'd be leaping into the aisle, trying to start another fight.

I throw my arm across his chest—a reflex—and he falls back, practically panting.

"Whoa, son," the man holds up his hands, leaning toward us all grinny like he wants to make up.

"Stop talking," I snap at him. "Just stop it. Leave us alone! We're not supposed to talk to strangers, you know."

The man looks injured. I've been so nice, and now I'm suddenly not. But I don't care. I glare at him, doing what I can to put the edge back around us. Me and Bailey on the inside. Him on the outside.

"Sure," he says, sliding his glasses back on. "Well, I hope you're not traveling far. By yourselves," he adds.

"We're fine."

"Uh-huh." He raises the newspaper again.

My arm is still stuck out straight, down across Bailey's middle. I pull it back; it's too weird to be touching so much of him.

Bailey gazes out the window. The hospital is long out of sight now, but I can tell he's still thinking about it. We're both still thinking about it when he reaches for my hand.

We lock our fingers and let them rest on the seat between us. Our palms touch only at the edges. In between is empty air, a little pocket. Just enough space for a secret or two.

Bailey turns his face away from the window after

a minute and leans his cheek against the headrest, like he's going to try to say something, but he doesn't manage anything.

"You don't have to tell me," I say.

"No?"

I understand everything now. Where he goes on Sundays. Why they might not have to move. Why maybe he wishes they would have to. Why he doesn't want to talk about it. When sad things happen, you build a room in your mind to put them. A safe place to hide the thoughts that make you want to cry. If you try really hard, you can sometimes get the door to lock.

But not always. I shrug. "I mean, you can tell me if you want to. . . ."

He shakes his head. "Maybe later."

We ride quietly, holding hands.

"I'm sorry," I say, even though I never really understand it when people say this to me. I guess it's just what you say at a time like this.

"I don't want anyone else to know," he whispers.

I have to kinda roll my eyes at that. "Who else do I talk to?"

He laughs softly. "Yeah, okay. We still gotta do something about that."

Chapter 48

THE BUS LETS US OFF AT THE STATION IN Las Vegas. It's so close to the Strip you can hear the water from the casino fountains rushing. That's good for us. The Mirage will be within walking distance.

"Have you been here?" Bailey says as we make our way toward the center of things. He follows my lead.

"Of course," I say. Grammie's brought me in a few times to look at the lights, plus sometimes we have school field trips to the museums and places like that.

"My mom and I drove around down here this weekend. We wanted to see everything."

"There's a lot to see."

"Yeah."

Bailey holds my hand as we cross the busy street. It's

funny to try to walk and hold hands at the same time. You've got to concentrate on two things at once—not getting hit by cars and not swinging your arm at the wrong pace.

We pick our way through the maze of traffic and emerge onto the Vegas Strip.

"Wow," Bailey says. "It looks different when you're not in a car."

The whole view is a little overwhelming. I glance around too, because no matter how many times I visit, I still think everything here looks way awesome. Giant statues in front of some casinos, fountains in front of others, and the boulevard strip down the center of the street is planted with palm trees.

It's not yet dark, but the sky has gone a dusky blue-gray. The night lights begin to flick on, gearing up to glow with full splendor when the sun goes down.

I can't remember where The Mirage is exactly, but it has to be close by. I start to lead us in the direction I think it is, but Bailey tugs my arm, holding me back. His other hand is warm, below the cap sleeve of my T-shirt. Until he touches me, I haven't realized how cool I am, how the desert breeze whirling around us has already stolen the heat of the day.

"I don't want you to think bad about me," Bailey says quietly.

I face him, squeezing his hand a little. "I don't. Why would you say that?"

No one else I know would have come on this crazy journey with me. Millie would be too scared. Under normal circumstances, even Z would have shied away from this unknown. I don't even know if I could have managed it by myself. It's bigger than anything I've ever tried to do, and yet Bailey didn't blink.

He's blinking now, though. Gripping my arm like there's no tomorrow. My heart starts pounding.

"What?" I say. If he freaks out now, then I'm going to freak out too. And that's no good for anybody.

Bailey looks away down the Strip. "My dad is sick." He hesitates.

"You don't have to tell me."

"Maybe I want to tell you," Bailey says. "Maybe I always wanted to."

"Okay."

"It's called post-traumatic stress disorder," Bailey says quietly. "He's just sick. He's not crazy."

I thumb toward the bus depot. "That guy on the bus was crazy."

Bailey smiles. "Yeah, totally." His smile fades, and I think I made a mistake by trying to be at all funny.

"He's going to get better," Bailey continues. "And—and

keklamagoon

he's really brave and he was in combat and everything, but . . . he never did the stuff I told the guys. At least, probably not." He looks away. "I don't know because he can't really talk about that kind of stuff. Sometimes he can't talk at all. . . ." Bailey's voice trails off.

"I get it," I say. "It's easier to make stuff up." There are other things I could say. Things that might let him see that I know how he feels. It's hard to be the broken one, the different one, the one carrying secrets and holding things that hurt.

"Yeah. Maybe." Bailey sighs. "Sometimes it's not so easy."

I take a deep breath, but it's hard because my heart is so full of him. "Let's go find Z."

Chapter 49

AS IT TURNS OUT, MY BEST GUESS ACTUALLY started us walking in the right direction. In a few moments we see the big neon signs on top of The Mirage glowing in the distance. We hurry toward it.

Out front, there's a massive rock volcano–sculpted fountain. The water flows over the wall of stones, then pools around the base in calm, sluicing waves. We follow the sidewalk around the zany decorations, scurrying beneath the canopy of palm trees that complete the oasis effect.

The Mirage itself looms above the coppice of trees like a giant open book. The entryway is beneath an arched dome. Through the glass doors, the hotel lobby gleams. Beyond it, the glint of shiny slot machines adds to the whole effect. It's a little bit blinding.

We plow through the doors, racing toward the casino floor. The *bling* and *ching* of the machines echo off of everything. We're encased in the quiet hum of people winning, losing, and placing the next bet.

We're moving so fast, we nearly bounce off the pair of security guys who step in front of us. Dressed in sleek gray suits, they're like two concrete pillars blocking our path.

"Not so fast," the tall one snaps. He catches me by the arm. His cohort plants a meaty hand on Bailey's shoulder. "No kids allowed."

"We're looking for someone," I protest. "We're not here to play."

"That's what they all say," the meaty bouncer mutters. "No parents, no entry."

"We're staying here," Bailey says, smoothing his charm over everything. I should have known to let him do the talking in the first place. He smiles. "Our parents are already inside."

The tall guy smiles back. "Then wait right here. We'll call up on the house phone. Room number?"

I glance at Bailey. His fibbing gears churn, but he draws up short, and so do I.

"Local brats," the meaty guy murmurs. They walk us to the door, briskly, roughly, spinning us out onto the concrete.

"It's getting late. Go home," the tall one snaps. The

glass doors slide shut behind us. We stand looking in, at the plush carpet, all the bright and flashing lights. So close and yet so far. On the other side, Tall and Meaty stand with arms crossed glaring down at us. There are a good six more of their buddies roaming in the background. These panes of glass might as well be the Great Wall of China.

Bailey and I glance at each other. Secret agent stealth or no—there's no way Z got past these guys.

"Where would he go?" Bailey says.

"This was your genius idea," I snap. How nuts am I being? I raced off to Vegas based on Bailey's random hunch. Z's probably been hiding in the automotive section eating stolen Pop-Tarts all this time. We are in so much trouble.

"Well, we can't keep standing here," Bailey says. He's right. Meaty raises his wrist to his mouth and speaks into his sleeve, still glaring at us.

"Let's go," I say. We retreat toward the fountain. "I can't believe I let you talk me into this."

Bailey cuts his eyes toward me. "I just had an idea," he says. "You were the one who ran for the bus station."

He's right, and I know it. I lean against the trunk of one of the decorative trees. "He said he had a mission. I should know where to look." My stomach starts to ache. Z's out there somewhere, alone. Maybe scared. *I'm* scared, and I'm with Bailey.

Bailey pulls the casino chip out of his pocket and flips it over, then strides toward the street. I push off the tree and follow. "What is it?"

Bailey gazes up and down the Strip. "They're all different," he says, "but kinda the same. If all he saw was a chip . . ."

"Okay, yeah." I get where he's going with this. A casino is a casino is a casino. If you strike out at one, you try another. I squinted my eyes, straining to put myself inside Z's head. Where would he go?

I scan the façades, thinking like Z. "That one." I point to the next casino along the same side of the street. Z wouldn't cross the boulevard if he didn't absolutely have to. Plus, it had a stony, classic look about it. Kind of like a castle.

"Okay, let's try that," Bailey says. We cross in front of the volcano, pushing past a small crowd that's gathered to gaze upon the attraction.

Bailey nudges me, chuckling. "Check it out. Rent-a-cop is talking to a bush."

Sure enough, several yards away, smack in the middle of the volcano's oasis, a Strip security guard stands with his fists planted on his cargo-belted hips speaking sternly toward a small shrub. He shakes a finger at it. Without warning, he reaches down, arm extended as if he's going to rip it out of the ground by the roots. The shriek that emanates from the bush is all too human, and all too familiar.

I run toward it.

Bailey was right all along. The Mirage.

"Don't touch him!" I shout. "Leave him alone."

The cop jerks back. I fly past him, and sure enough, there is Z. Hunched in a tiny ball with his backpack all askew at his side. Clutching his Altoids box with the rubber bands, his special secret box. Out in the open. Tears are streaming down his face.

I kneel in front of him. He flinches away when I try to touch him. "Hey, it's just me," I whisper, drawing my hand back. "Zachariah?"

I wait for the usual "Milady," but it doesn't come.

"Hey, girlie," the rent-a-cop says. "You know this kid?"

"We know him," Bailey says. "He's our friend. He wandered away from the group."

"What group?" The cop reaches for his walkie-talkie.

Bailey puts up a hand to delay him. "Our school group. We've been at the museums all day. We were just headed back to the buses when this one wandered off." Bailey rolls his eyes and rambles on about the museum and the teachers and the "day" we've had in town.

I'm shocked by Bailey's tale. It swirls over my head, and I'm glad the cop is drawn into it, so I don't have to try to explain anything myself. I press my hand on the curb while I move my legs to get more comfortable.

"Zachariah, it's me. Eleanor. The quest is over. It's time to go home. Our horses are waiting in the stable." I whisper the story to him.

Z's crying doesn't seem to be slowing down. I thought, once he saw me, he'd know everything was going to be okay. But I'm not sure he's seeing me or knows it's really me.

Bailey talks on and on. "Anyway, our teachers are coming. Any second now."

The cop looks down the street, uncertain. "You sure?"

"Yeah, yeah," Bailey says smoothly. "They're right behind us. We ran ahead 'cause we were worried about our friend."

I narrow my eyes at him. The lies that bubble up seem to come easy. But I don't have time right now to wonder about Bailey's tales.

"You don't even have to wait with us," Bailey continues. "Really. We're fine. We have supervision."

The cop glances at me. I smile, which I hope he will take as confirmation of Bailey's story.

"Sure, okay," he says after a moment. "No problem. You kids take care now." He claps Bailey's shoulder and takes two steps back, then turns to leave.

Bailey grins at me, triumphant. But I shake my head.

As he walks slowly away, the cop reaches for his walkie-talkie. He mumbles something into it.

Bailey may be a smooth talker, but he's no kind of miracle worker. We're not out of the woods just yet.

Chapter 50

"WELL, THIS IS A FULL-ON SNAFU," Bailey says, moments later.

"What?" I whisper. The last ninety seconds were easily the most terrifying of my entire life. I'm still trying to recover.

First the volcano erupts. Flashing, hissing, red flowing lava explodes onto the sky all around us, rushing in rivers where moments before the cool fountain waters had been lapping calmly. Z screams. I scream. Bailey dives on top of us like he can protect us with his body, but all that happens is we all three end up ground into the mulch under Z's bush.

Then The Mirage security team appears, four huge gray columns of them. Tall, Meaty, and their friends BuzzCut and Knuckles. Plus the original rent-a-cop, who must have thought he was so clever, walking away to call for backup just before the volcanic light show began at its appointed hour.

When the eruption's over, the crowd gathered around the volcano bursts into applause. But their cheering stalls when Z's shrieking continues in earnest, no longer covered by the explosive entertainment display. The security guys bear down on us. Two lift Bailey up off us. One grabs me and another scoops up Z, who curls into a ball in his arms like a baby. Bailey struggles against their hold. I don't see the point. They have us good.

"Congratulations," Meaty mutters over my head. "You just bought your ticket inside."

Bailey fights it all the way. They've got him by the arms, and he drags his feet like he's being hauled to his execution. "You can't do this!" he shouts. "Just 'cause we're kids. We still got rights!"

We're through the lobby in a matter of moments. They sweep us right past the glitz, through a dingy, cement-lined hallway, into a small receiving room with chairs.

The second room they open is small and maybe soundproofed. When they put Z inside and close the door, his cries fade to almost nothing.

"No," I blurt. "I need to be in there with him." Meaty glances at BuzzCut and shrugs. They open the door and push us inside.

The door slams. It's the three of us, alone. Trapped somewhere in The Mirage. With no way out.

"Situation Normal All Funked Up," Bailey murmurs in explanation. "Snafu. In the army they don't say 'funked,' but I'm not supposed to curse."

I glance at him out of the corner of my eye. We're about to die at the hands of the gestapo and he's worried about foul language?

Z sobs from the middle of the floor, huddled where Tall must have deposited him. His distress takes precedence over our little imprisonment dilemma. Together, we approach him.

"What are we going to do?" I say.

"I don't know," Bailey says, "but we have to try something."

Z rocks back and forth, cupping his ears. He's a tiny ball of terror, and I don't know how to touch him.

Bailey sits down on the carpet.

"Hey, man."

I kneel close to Z. I wish I knew what had happened to him today. Then maybe I would know what to say. Maybe I could find the right words to help him pretend it was all better.

"Zachariah?" I reach for his hand. He flinches.

I drop my head onto my knees. I should have been with

him. If I'd been paying attention, I would have been there. I would have gone with him, held his hand while his world fell apart. I owe him that.

"Do we know what's in the box?" Bailey asks. It's trapped between Z's thighs and belly.

"Not that one. No, don't—"

But Bailey reaches for it, manages to free it. My heart pounds hard and harder. It's wrong, all wrong. Z doesn't let anyone touch his boxes, ever. But he's frozen, staring at whatever horror is in front of him. Wrong, all wrong.

"What happened to him?" Bailey says. "What happened to make him like this?"

"It's just who he is," I say.

Bailey shakes his head. "He's . . . broken."

"Don't say that!" I shout. "You don't know him. You don't know us. We're fine."

"Yeah," Bailey murmurs. "This is so fine."

It's not, it's not, but I've been protecting Z for so long, I don't know any other way. "I thought you were different," I say. "I thought you weren't like the others, always saying there's something wrong. Sometimes people are just different. Did you ever think of that?"

"Ella." Bailey looks tormented. Z's whimpers are pitiful and loud. "He needs help. We have to help him."

"We're fine."

"What happened to him?"

I shake my head.

"I know you know. Just tell me."

I see Z, huddled, crying. And I know Bailey's right. It's not a game anymore. It's not a moment in a tree house. It's not a gift to me or a fantasy to pop in and out of. It's become everything to Z. And it's eating him up.

"His dad left," I blurt. "They lost their house. It was horrible for him."

Z suddenly falls silent. The air echoes with nothingness. He's been listening. He hears me.

Bailey nods at me to keep talking. He tugs off the rubber bands and pops Z's box open, sifting through whatever's inside. Part of me wants to look too. But I don't.

"His mom works at Walmart. I'm pretty sure they sleep there now. They don't have anywhere to go."

After a while Bailey closes the lid.

"They need money," I tell Bailey. "I think he saw the chips and realized they were money. I think he wanted to steal some."

"No," Bailey says. "He's looking for his dad."

"What?" That doesn't make any sense.

Bailey tips the box toward me. The contents are a jumble, but they answer the question. Photographs of Z and his dad. A postcard from Seattle. A tie clip with a horseshoe.

A marble. A pocketknife. A book of matches. A Universal Studios keychain. Small objects that speak of Z's dad and all that they shared.

I slide aside the photos and draw a slow breath. Three casino chips from The Mirage. Z's dad used to gamble, like Grammie, but a lot more often. Did he give these to Z? Did he come to The Mirage? Was this where he lost the money that should have paid for their home? The pieces fall together in my mind.

"There are more where these came from."

"The quest begins today."

Bailey's right. Z's looking for his dad. Looking for the answers that aren't coming.

"It's hard," I say. "When someone you love leaves and you know they're never coming back. You start to forget things about them, and it's terrible. You just want to go somewhere else."

I'm talking about Z. And I'm talking about me. Bailey sits, listening, and somehow I know I'm talking about him, too. I keep telling him he doesn't know us, but maybe he does.

"It's really sad," I say. "People who leave . . . they don't come back."

"Don't tell him that," Bailey says. "It's not true."

His voice is firm. He believes what he's saying.

What if his dad gets better? Then he'd get out of the hospital and they could keep moving. Bailey will be happy, but he'll have to leave. And what if Z's dad comes home? He'll move to a new house and won't need to pretend anymore. Then I'll be all alone.

I've tried to get Z to understand what I do—that when people leave they don't come back. Still, he believes. He believes hard enough to run here, looking for his own kind of perfect.

Mine is never coming back. I want to go back to the time when everything was right around me. Back before I figured out that the way my face looks equals ugly. Back when Millie wore braids, and Z knew the difference between the real world and a dream, when Mom lived at home seven days out of seven and Dad kissed my cheeks every night at bedtime. When Z's magic was just magic and not something so horribly wrong.

My eyes are crying and my heart is crying. Three years ago today I started forgetting him. But you're not supposed to forget. You're supposed to remember. Forever.

When nothing is perfect, it's just easier to hide.

"You lied," I say to Bailey. "You made me believe we're the same."

"I didn't lie to you," he says. "I didn't have to. We are the same."

We sit there, and I just look at him for a while, because I simply don't see it. And then, out of nowhere, I do.

I am Camo-Face. Invisible in plain sight. Not wanting to be seen. Hiding from the sad truth of things. That Daddy is gone. That Z is broken. But these things I hide from are huge now, so huge that they can't be hidden, not even by a giant lava-spewing volcano.

Bailey hides behind popularity, and lies. He's like us, but different. He knows how to be out in the world. He knows how to pretend in a way that makes him likable, not weird.

I see it now, how we're the same. We are all camouflaged.

Chapter 51

WITHOUT Z'S CRIES, THE ROOM IS quiet.

"Do you think he's okay now?" Bailey says.

Z lies curled on the floor. His damp eyelashes rest against his cheeks, as if he's fallen asleep. But he's breathing too hard to be less than awake.

"Yeah, maybe," I say.

"We gotta try to get out of here." Bailey gets up and bangs on the metal door.

Tall opens the door. "The cops will be here in a minute," he says.

"We didn't do anything wrong," Bailey says.

Tall shrugs. "Doesn't matter. You're unaccompanied

minors, and there's no reason for you to be wandering the Strip alone at night."

Bailey protests, but Tall is having none of it. Z's quiet now, so he leaves the door to the room open. I lie on the floor beside Z, trying to prepare him for what's about to happen.

"Agent Z," I whisper. "We've completed stage one of the mission. We've infiltrated the fortress."

After a moment Z sits up. "Yes, yes," he says. He slinks along the floor until his back is pressed against the wall. He glances furtively left and right, before reaching for his things.

Z hums quietly to himself, hugging his backpack, his boxes. His world is right again. The walls are back in place and it's business as usual. The only difference is, I can now see how un-right it is. How un-right it has been all along. I take his hand, trying to think of what to say to him. How to tell him that it's time for the game to be over. I let it go on too long. I thought we could handle it, just between us, but we can't. Not anymore.

Chapter 52

THE POLICE STATION IS DINGY AND GROSS. The paint is peeling, and several chairs are broken, and there's a lot of gum stuck to things. Everything about Las Vegas looks sparkly clean on the outside but really isn't when you get right down to it.

We're in major trouble, but we didn't break the law, so we're not under arrest or anything. They let us sit in the waiting room. Our moms are on their way, the desk officer tells us.

We're a little keyed up, so we don't really sit right away. We walk around looking at things on the walls. A poster about how to do CPR. A DARE poster. A row of pamphlets about things like preventing home invasion and how to cope with crime if it happens to you. A dispenser of hand sanitizer.

I'm scrubbing the germs off my hands with a dollop of foam when an older woman, round of body but barely taller than Bailey, whips around the corner and plows straight into me, practically knocking me over. Her purse straps fall off her shoulder into the crook of her arm. A scarf drifts to the floor from somewhere.

"Where did you come from?" she barks at me. "You weren't there a second ago."

"Uh—," I say.

"Excuse yourself," the lady insists. "And watch where you're going, young lady."

"Uh—" Is it rude to mention that I was standing perfectly still? "You ran into me," I say, indignant.

The woman fixes hawk eyes upon us, as if we are exactly the sort of young ruffians that populate her worst nightmares.

"Our fault, ma'am," Bailey rushes to say. "We weren't looking. Are you quite all right?"

"Yes, yes, fine. But—"

Bailey offers that fabulous grin. "We're here to report a terrible crime," he says. "We're witnesses, and, well, we're quite upset. We're just not ourselves at the moment. I'm sure you understand."

The woman smooths her shirt. "Well, yes, I'm sure . . ." She trails off. I'm still impressed that Bailey has the presence of mind to defuse a weird situation on the spur of the moment.

Z bends over and collects her scarf. He bows courtly as he passes it to her. "A good day to you, milady."

She straightens her purse and wanders off, muttering something about kids today.

I start to laugh. I can't help it.

We're a ridiculous trio. Z, the pretender. Bailey, the liar. Me, the invisible. The camo-faced girl who no one really sees.

I know it's not really a time for laughing. Bailey glances at me, concerned. I try to explain.

"We—" I'm gasping for breath through my hysterics. "We are such total freaks!"

"Freaks," Z repeats. "Freaks!" he shouts.

I crack up completely, stumbling toward a row of chairs. I bury my face in my knees until I can breathe again.

The guys settle on either side of me. I sense them there, Bailey on my left, Z on my right. After a minute Bailey puts his hand on my back, and that's how I can tell that we do know each other, a little. It's how I can tell he knows that laughing is what I have to do right now to get through it.

When I've got my breath back, I hug Z with one arm. "We're going to fix it," I tell him. I plop a tiny kiss on his cheek, which he rubs away automatically with the back of his hand. I know he hears me.

camogirl

203

I catch Bailey's eye and try to put away the part of me that's embarrassed. It doesn't quite work. My face goes warm.

"Can I—" Bailey stops. "Can I have one too?"

There's this quiet moment of us looking at each other, then we both lean in. My heart races and I hold my breath as our lips touch, just a little. We pull back right away, and open our eyes. Bailey smiles, but I don't know if I did the kiss right, and my mouth wants to go again. In the movies they press all up against each other, so I try that the second time, and my nose flattens onto his cheek. It's not terrible.

"Freaks," Z murmurs again, out of nowhere. We back away.

I'm not sure I want to look at him now, but Bailey just shrugs. Grins. "What happens in Vegas . . . ," he murmurs.

Smiling, too, I stick out my hand and we shake on it.

Chapter 53

AILEY'S MOM REACHES US FIRST. "GROUNDED beyond grounded, mister," Mrs. James says, even as she grabs Bailey and hugs him, prodding him all over to be sure he's still in one piece.

Mom and Lynn aren't far behind. We don't really do grounding in my house, but I can tell by the expression on Mom's face that I'm in for a long, firm talking-to. Bailey got the better end of that deal, as far as I'm concerned. At least when you're grounded they basically leave you alone.

Lynn is super lenient with Z, if you ask me, but then again, he's not really in a position to appreciate punishment. She just scoops him into her arms and whispers, "Don't scare me like that. Don't go away, okay?" He wraps his skinny arms around her neck and doesn't let go for a long time.

Mom and Mrs. James shake hands, meeting for the first time. "Roberta James," Bailey's mom says.

"Of course. Keisha Cartwright," Mom says. They shake their heads about us and our antics, teaming up against us.

It's totally weird. Bailey and I glance at each other. I wonder if he's feeling the same as me—like something special's suddenly over. Our secret little life.

Mom goes to the counter to talk to the police officers who brought us over from the casino. Mrs. James pulls out her car keys and hands them to Bailey. "Go wait for me in the car."

Bailey tosses me a last, desperate glance before heading for the door, a condemned man.

"It was all my idea," I tell Mrs. James, because it looks like Bailey's about to be in a lot of trouble.

Mrs. James smiles. She smooths back my hair on one side, kind of the way my mom does sometimes. "You're a sweet girl, Ella. And you clearly care a lot about your friends. But let me tell you something, okay?" she says. "You have to stop feeling responsible for other people's actions. Let Bailey take care of Bailey, and you just take care of you."

I nod as if I understand. I guess she's right. Bailey figured out The Mirage, so it was partly his idea. And anyway, he didn't have to come along. That's for sure.

I follow Mrs. James to the desk, where I lean against Mom, up under her arm, while she fills out some paperwork so we can go home.

In the car, Mom cries behind the wheel for the second time today. We don't even make it out of the station parking lot. Lynn reaches across the console for her hand.

"I'm sorry, Lynn," Mom says. "I can't believe I didn't see it. It's so hard not being here."

The lesson of the day is: Z is not okay. The thing I knew deep down is on the surface now, with no place to hide.

I look at him across the backseat. His boxes are neatly packed away, but he holds his backpack on his lap. He gazes out the window, and I wonder if he's trying to make sense of things or if he's already put it away in his mind.

I tug on the strap of my seat belt for no good reason. Just for something to do.

After a minute Mom and Lynn shake off the tears and we go. They talk quietly in the front seat, in the grown-up way, but I listen. I listen, because Mom has a plan.

Tonight, Z will sleep at Millie's house, in the spare bedroom. We don't have one ourselves, so Mom's already called Mrs. Taylor to make it okay. In the morning Mom and Lynn will take Z to a meeting with a doctor who Mom says maybe can help him. The bad news is, he might have to go away after that. He needs a place to live, Mom says, wherever that is, as hard as it will be for all of us. For Lynn. For Z. For me.

I close my eyes and lean back. Mom knows what to do. Mom can help. Maybe I won't have to work so hard, worry so hard. I hold the seat belt strap, certain it's all that's holding me down. I feel so light. Something huge has been lifted off me, and it's going to be okay.

Chapter 54

RAMMIE SPRINGS OUT OF HER CHAIR TO greet us. "Well, that was quite a stunt you pulled, missy." She flaps her arms a bit and ends up hugging me.

"Hey," I say. "If you're going to get in trouble, you might as well do it big."

Grammie chuckles. "Well, this was a whopper. And you must be starving."

Now that you mention it . . .

We sit down to eat, one of Grammie's crazy concoctions. Let's call it Casserole X.

After dinner we retreat to the living room to let things settle. Grammie puts the news on low, and I sprawl on the floor and pull out my homework. I've almost finished social studies when the TV suddenly goes silent. I glance up.

"Come here," Mom says from the couch. "Right this minute."

Uh-oh. It's time for the talking-to. Mom's face is so stiff that I go to her. I'm much too big for lap sitting, but she drags me onto her anyway, hugging me like there's no tomorrow.

"It was a good thing you did," she says. "Really brave, going after him like that."

"But you're still in trouble," Grammie pipes up from her chair.

Mom kisses my face. "Yes, you are." She gets all serious on me and pushes her forehead against mine. "Do you know you can talk to us?" she whispers. "About anything. Anything you're ever worried about, even just a little?"

"Yes," I say, because I do know, but everyone makes mistakes. I thought I was protecting Z. Helping him. I thought it was the right thing to do.

"Well, good," Grammie says. "But that's beside the point." She slams her recliner closed, and juts a finger at me. "Under no circumstances whatsoever do you run off to Vegas with a boy. Any boy. Ever. Is that clear?"

"Geez, Grammie. We didn't get married," I grumble. "We just held hands."

"Lordy Lou," Grammie shrieks. "Keisha, we've got to move!"

Mom laughs, and for a second I'm convinced I'm getting off easy. Then they lay it on me. A long list of chores and a suspension of my allowance. Apparently noble intentions don't count for much around here.

Chapter 55

'M ALL READY FOR BED WHEN I GLANCE OUT THE window, purely by accident. Then I look again, to be sure I'm seeing what I see. Millie and Z, making their way toward the tree house.

I can't help myself. I slide into a pair of shoes and before I know it, I'm gliding across the grass. I reach them just as Z disappears over the ledge into the tree house. Millie and I meet at the base of the rope ladder.

"What are you doing?" I snap. It's just the backyard. The tree house. So why does it feel like trouble? Like a violation of *us*. "Is he okay?"

"He wouldn't stop looking out the window at it," Millie says. "So, I thought . . ." She fingers the hem of her pajama top and gazes uncertainly at me.

"Oh. That's good," I say, relaxing somewhat. "You did the right thing."

Then there's a moment when we're both just standing there, realizing something. We're each wearing the pink and purple polka-dot pajamas we bought last year so we could match at slumber parties. Funny how I forgot we did that.

We look at each other and smile. For the first time in a long time, we know what the other's thinking.

"Now what?" Millie says.

"Now I go up to sit with him. You can go back to bed." I put my feet on the bottom rope rung. But Millie doesn't leave. "Or you can come up," I offer. It's her tree house, after all.

Millie smiles again. Her hair is loosely braided on either side of head. It's not a friend thing. It's because she sleeps on her back and it feels comfortable. I know that in the morning she'll brush it out into a glossy ponytail that I can never copy, but right now I feel good. Because all I can think is, *I know you on the inside.*

We climb. Z sits in the tree house center, drumming on a pillow with his fists. "Ellie-nor," he murmurs.

"What are you doing?" I whisper to him. "It's late."

He doesn't answer, but I know the tree house has

always been a favorite place for him. A safe place, where no one goes but us. He drums hard, the way he always does something with his hands when he's nervous or excited or worried.

That's when I realize he knows. Tonight isn't just another night. Tomorrow won't be just another day. It's the beginning of the end of something. Something amazing and special that we share. After this the world tilts back toward ordinary, and what kind of a life will that be?

"Zachariah," I say, taking his frenzied hand. "Everything's about to get so much better."

"Better," he repeats. "Better, better, better . . ."

A chill breeze stirs the leaves, swirling around us as if conjured by Z's mumbled chant. We shiver, not dressed for the night. Z lies down and tucks into a ball.

"We can't sleep here," Millie says. "We don't have our sleeping bags."

"Yeah."

But Z's busy cozying himself among the pillows.

"Brave knight," I say. "The fair lady Millicent must return to her castle, across the cold dark plain. Not a safe journey to make alone."

Z's eyelids flutter sleepily, but he can't resist the call. "I will escort her, milady."

We descend one by one, and I walk with them to Millie's

back door. I want to grab Z and hug him, but he would protest. So I curtsy.

"Good night, Sir Zachariah."

"Good night," he murmurs. "Good night, fair Ellie-nor."

I wonder if he knows good night really means good-bye. Good-bye for now, anyway. I touch the screen as the door closes behind Z.

I want to see him the rest of the way, but I can't. He needs something else now, something more than what I can give. And I love him enough to let him go.

Chapter 56

I WAKE IN THE MORNING, KNOWING WHAT I HAVE TO do. Today must be the final ride of the Lady Eleanor.

I glance at the photo of Daddy, like I do every day. His smile gives me courage like nothing else could. It's Year Four, Day One, and I am ready.

I slide my toes out from under the covers, feeling for the golden stirrups that await me. I mount my steed with casual elegance, tossing back my unruly mane of glorious curls. I gallop around the room for a minute, getting a feel for things.

I've decided there has to be a certain amount of ceremony to it. After all, I've lived with Lady Eleanor off and on for three years, and every day of the past year she's made an appearance. It's not super easy to put all that aside.

I pause before entering the hallway. It's hard to imagine a world without Z, which is where I'm going to be living for a while. Maybe forever, because when he comes back, he'll be his real self. I have to be ready.

The trusty horse carries me, eyes wide open, into the bathroom. In front of the mirror I dismount, with a flourish. I take a deep breath, let the cape fall away, and stare into the face of me, Ella.

I step close and closer, lean across the counter to get a good look.

This is my face forever.

This is the face I'll be wearing when I walk to the bus stop. The face I'll be wearing when I finally get to eat lunch with Millie and her friends. The face I'll wear to meet Bailey at the basketball hoop, whenever his grounding is over. The face that Z will be looking for when he finally comes home.

I thought it was easier to close my eyes. To make believe that hiding would make it all better. The truth is, there's no way to hide. Bailey knows what I look like, and Millie, and Z. They like me anyway.

I stare at myself hard and harder, but blinking gets in the way. Every time I come back, I see something different. I see light brown, dark brown. I see ugly. I see camo. I see eyes, nose, mouth. I see blotches. Camo. Brown. Ugly. Eyes.

Camo. Mouth. There . . . something else . . . just for a second. I try to get it back, but I can't.

I lean away, reaching for my toothbrush, still looking. Always looking. Ella, the girl in the mirror. Camo. Brown. Skin. Face. That other thing, that elusive thing, it comes and goes, still trying to come out of hiding.

"Anyone who can see will see you beautiful," Mom always says. Maybe, just maybe, I'm starting to see.